ACCLAIM FOR THE NOVELS OF OPAL CAREW

"A blazing hot erotic romp . . . a must-read for lovers of erotic romance. A fabulously fun and stupendously steamy read for a cold winter's night. This one's so hot, you might need to wear oven mitts while you're reading it!"
—*Romance Junkies*

4 stars! "Carew's devilish twists and turns keep the emotional pitch of the story moving from sad to suspenseful to sizzling to downright surprising in the end. . . . The plot moves swiftly and satisfyingly."
—*RT Book Reviews*

"Fresh, exciting, and extremely sexual with characters you'll fall in love with. Absolutely fantastic!"
—*Fresh Fiction*

"The constant and imaginative sexual situations keep the reader's interest along with likable characters with emotional depth. Be prepared for all manner of coupling, including groups, exhibitionism, voyeurism, and same sex unions. . . . I recommend *Swing* for the adventuresome who don't mind singeing their senses."
—*Regency Reader*

"Carew pulls off another scorcher . . . she knows how to write a love scene that takes her reader to dizzying heights of pleasure."
—*My Romance Story*

"So much fun to read . . . The story line is fast-paced with wonderful humor."
—*Genre Go Round Reviews*

"A great book . . . Ms. Carew has wonderful imagination."
—*Night Owl Romance Reviews*

"Opal Carew brings erotic romance to a whole new level . . . she writes a compelling romance and sets your senses on fire with her love scenes!"
—*Reader to Reader*

ALSO BY OPAL CAREW

Secret Ties

Six

Blush

Swing

Twin Fantasies

Forbidden Heat

Opal Carew

St. Martin's Griffin

New York

FORBIDDEN HEAT. Copyright © 2009 by Elizabeth
Batten-Carew. All rights reserved. Printed in the United States
of America. For information, address St. Martin's Press, 175 Fifth
Avenue, New York, N.Y. 10010.

www.stmartins.com

Library of Congress Cataloging-in-Publication Data

Carew, Opal.
   Forbidden heat / Opal Carew. — 1st ed.
      p.   cm.
   ISBN 978-0-312-58013-1
  1. Bisexual men—Fiction.   2. Group sex–Fiction.
3. Triangles (Interpersonal relations)—Fiction.   I. Title.
   PR9199.4.C367F67 2010
813'.6—dc22

                       2009039993

First Edition: January 2010

10 9 8 7 6 5 4 3 2 1

To Jason,
who is always
true to himself,

and

to Jenn,
who is the daughter
I never had

Acknowledgments

As always, my hearty thanks go out to my wonderful editor, Rose Hilliard. Every one of my books is better because of her insights and ideas. Thanks to my fabulous agent, Emily Sylvan Kim, who provides ideas, support, and encouragement. It is a pleasure to work with both of you. Thanks to my husband, Mark, who supports me in so many ways, including essential technical support to keep my computer and Internet connection functioning, but mostly because of his loving encouragement and his charming ways! Finally, thanks to my two sons, whose very presence raises my happiness level.

One

Danielle Rayne wheeled her suitcase into the elevator and turned around. As the doors closed, her gaze caught on two tall, attractive men, one with short tousled sandy blond hair and one with light brown hair neatly tied back in a pony-tail. They were crossing the hotel lobby toward the reception desk, both stylishly dressed in slim-fit jeans.

Oh my God. Trey and Jake.

The two men she had fantasized about for almost fifteen years. Two men who had haunted her dreams. Kissing her. Holding her. Her cheeks flushed as hot, sweaty images from those dreams rippled through her mind.

The older woman standing beside her glanced her way. "Are you okay?" she asked, kind blue eyes taking in Danielle's burning crimson cheeks.

"Yes, fine thank you. Just a bit of a cold coming on," she lied.

Danielle took a deep breath and tried to steady her racing heart. As much as she yearned to be with Jake . . . or Trey . . . or *both* . . . it would never be. Because Jake and Trey were in love . . . with each other.

At least, they used to be. When she knew them in college.

Were they still together? They had arrived at the hotel together. Of course, that wasn't such a surprise. A lot of the old gang would be here. Danielle had flown to Buffalo to attend her old friend Harmony's wedding.

Old friend? Well, more like an acquaintance now. She and Harmony could have had a close friendship, but Danielle hadn't kept in touch, even though Harmony had tried for a while. She'd sent e-mails, Christmas cards, letters.

Danielle had always intended to write her back, but never seemed to get around to it. Eventually Harmony's e-mails and cards tapered off, and then stopped completely.

Danielle didn't mean to sabotage her chances at friendship, but somehow, by inattentiveness, she always seemed to manage it. Well, no use beating herself up about it. She was here now and that was all that mattered.

The elevator doors opened on the fifteenth floor. She smiled at the lady beside her and stepped from the elevator, then pulled her suitcase behind her down the long hallway toward her room.

"You're in room 1512, Mr. Garner. I hope you enjoy your stay."

Trey glanced at the lovely desk clerk's name tag, and then returned her smile with an added wink. "Thank you, Georgia."

Her cheeks flushed slightly.

Jake nudged Trey's arm as they stepped away from the desk. "Stop flirting with the poor woman," he said with a grin. "You know it's not going to go anywhere."

"Why do you think that?" Trey asked as they approached the elevator.

"Well, for one reason, because we've already made plans for tonight."

Trey pushed the elevator call button. "Sure, but then there's tomorrow."

He glanced across the lobby at the lovely blonde Georgia as she consulted her computer. She swept her long waves of silky hair back over her shoulder, then glanced up to see his gaze directed at her. She smiled luminously, then returned her gaze to her current client, but Trey could tell the woman was interested. Very interested.

"And who knows . . . maybe Georgia would be interested in joining us tonight."

Jake chuckled. The elevator doors whooshed open and he followed Trey inside. He pushed the button for their floor, then the doors closed and the elevator began to move.

"Nice of you to share, but surely you can do without a woman for one night. I thought we'd do some catching up."

Trey grinned and shrugged. "Well, I guess I could try. But just 'cause we're such good friends."

The doors opened and Jake exited the elevator, followed by Trey.

"Down this way," Jake said as he headed left down the hallway. "I think they're the two at the end of the hall."

Danielle unzipped the vinyl cover and removed the aqua dress she intended to wear to the wedding tomorrow, then hung it in the closet. She heard male voices in the hall and went to the door and peered out the peephole. Jake and Trey walked by her room.

Good heavens, they were on the same floor. In fact, since hers was the second-to-last room from the end, they must be in the room next to hers, or across the hall from that one.

They were definitely still together, Danielle decided. They'd arrived together and now it seemed they were in the same room. She smiled. They had been so in love in college, and that had had a big impact on her. She heard a door open, then click closed.

Although she would love it if the men were free and

single . . . *and liked women* . . . it made her heart swell to think that their relationship could last so long. She hadn't experienced much of that . . . relationships that lasted. Nothing in her life had been stable, and the thought that someone else could make a go of a relationship, could actually find another person to depend on, to love, and who loved him back . . . it made her feel a little better about the world.

Trey crossed the lobby toward the lounge, then stepped into the dimly lit room and glanced around. When he'd called Jake to see if he was ready for dinner, Jake had needed another twenty minutes for a shower, so Trey had said he'd wait for him here.

"Hey there."

Trey glanced around to see a woman with long flowing blond hair behind him.

"Hello, Georgia. You look lovely this evening."

She'd changed from her uniform into a halter-style floral dress. The form-fitting bodice set off her slim figure. She was sexy and feminine, and definite interest sparkled in her grayish blue eyes. He was interested, too, but he'd promised to spend the evening with Jake.

"I just got off work and . . . when I saw you heading in here, I wondered if we could grab a drink together? Maybe dinner, if you're free?"

"I'm meeting a friend for dinner, but . . ." He smiled

5

and took her hand, then kissed it. "I could join you for a quick drink."

Jake entered the lounge and saw Trey sitting at a table in the corner. Jake's heart still clenched whenever he saw Trey. His warm brown eyes that glittered with golden specks, his strong square jaw, his full sensual lips . . . even the glint of his diamond earring . . . all reminded Jake of what he'd lost when Trey had decided to shift their relationship to one of friends rather than lovers. And the friendship had worked for the years they'd been in college when they'd shared a town house with Angela and Nikki, but now . . . They lived in the same town—even worked at the same place— yet hardly saw each other. Jake just found it too hard to see Trey and not be with him.

As Jake walked across the room, a young woman with blond hair approached Trey's table and sat down, setting her purse on a spare chair. Georgia from reception. Jake noticed two drinks on the table.

Georgia said something to Trey and he laughed; then he glanced up and saw Jake approach the table.

"Jake, you remember Georgia."

"Of course." He smiled, but inside, jealousy swirled through him. Trey would no doubt have chosen to spend a casual evening of sex with this woman if Jake hadn't already booked the evening with him.

And why not? She was beautiful and sexy. Hell, if Trey hadn't been interested in her, Jake would have been. After all, there was no reason either one of them shouldn't pursue an attractive woman. It wasn't like there was anything between Jake and Trey anymore.

Trey had totally moved on, Jake reminded himself, and dwelling on what might have been was a recipe for heartache.

"Well, it's time for me to be off." Trey signed the check on the table.

"Do you have to leave so soon?" she asked.

Trey smiled. "Sorry, honey." He took Georgia's hand and kissed it. "But I had a delightful time."

She smiled, but couldn't keep the disappointment from her face. Trey was such a lady's man.

"Have a good time at the wedding tomorrow," she said as they walked toward the door.

They stepped outside into the warm evening.

"I'll get us a cab," Jake said. "Any ideas where to go for dinner?"

"Georgia suggested we go to a little Italian restaurant just a block down, so we can walk."

They turned left and strolled down the street and a few minutes later entered a classy Italian restaurant.

"Please, follow me," the mustached host said as he led them through a maze of hallways passing small groupings of tables in intimate niches along the way. "Is this to your liking?" he asked when he stopped at a booth in a niche of its own.

"Great. Thanks."

"Could you bring us a carafe of your house wine? Our friend told us to be sure and try it," Trey said.

"Right away." The man hurried off, leaving them to enjoy the soft dinner music playing in the background.

"Nice atmosphere." Jake picked up one of the menus the host had set on the table.

The waiter arrived with a carafe of red wine, two stemmed glasses, and a basket of fresh-baked bread. He set the bread on the table, then filled the glasses. Both Trey and Jake ordered the house specialty. The waiter scooped up the menus and went on his way.

"So what's going on with you these days?" Trey asked.

"Since we're into the summer session, I have a pretty light class load."

Trey nodded. "Got the pool open?"

"Of course. You're welcome to come over for a dip anytime."

"Yeah, sure," Trey said. "I'll have to do that."

But Jake knew it wouldn't happen. Besides, he'd forgotten that Trey had a pool of his own.

The waiter arrived with their salads.

"What about you?" Jake asked.

"I went on a forty-mile ride last month."

"Yeah? That's not too long for you." As long as Jake had known him, Trey had been an avid cyclist and often did lengthy trips.

"True, but Lindsay . . . the woman I went with . . . hadn't done a ride that long before, so we had to ease into it."

"Hmm." Jake grinned. "A woman willing to go into training to be with you. Sounds serious."

Trey shrugged. "I thought so, but . . . no. She ended it a week later." He took a bite of his salad.

At the haunted look in Trey's eyes, Jake's heart compressed. He'd obviously cared about the woman. "Sorry to hear that."

"No problem. That's just me . . . looking for love in all the wrong places. Just because we shared a few interests didn't mean it was a match made in heaven. Our personalities didn't mesh well together."

Jake had gotten the sense for a long time now that Trey had decided to leave his interest in men completely behind him and hoped to find a woman to settle down with. Start a family. Have a *normal* life . . . at least, one he didn't feel he had to hide.

"What about you?" Trey asked. "I heard you were dating Rachel in the science department."

"For a while . . . but that ended in April. Before that, I was seeing a guy named Rico." It felt strange talking to

Trey about his love life, but he tamped down the awkward feelings. After all, friends talked about their love lives all the time, didn't they?

"I heard that became a bit of a problem." Trey grabbed a slice of bread from the basket and buttered it.

Jake pushed back stray strands of hair that had escaped his ponytail. Trey seemed to know a lot about his relationships. Was that friendly interest, or could it be more?

"Yeah. The guy was pretty emotional . . . and overly possessive. I finally had to end it."

Trey nodded. "It's tough out there. Finding the right person. Making a go of it. If you do find the right person, though, I'm sure it's worth the effort."

"I wouldn't know," Jake said, shifting his gaze to the bread as he picked up a slice and buttered it. "What about you? Do you think you ever will?"

"I hope so," Trey said with a shrug. "Enough about this, though." Trey grinned. "So tomorrow, Harmony ties the knot."

Jake nodded. Harmony had found someone she loved and whom she would spend her life with. She was proof it could be done.

Jake glanced at Trey. If only he could find someone in his life who thought he was special . . . who would make him forget how much he wanted Trey.

"It'll be great seeing a lot of old friends tomorrow," Jake said.

Trey leaned forward. "You know who we haven't seen for a long time? Remember Danielle Rayne from first year? I wonder if she'll be there."

"I'm sure. She and Harmony were pretty close friends."

Danielle had transferred to another school after first year. Financial considerations.

Trey leaned back in his chair. "Remember I had kind of a thing for her?"

Jake remembered. In fact, he had, too. But then Jake had always known he was interested in both men and women. For Trey, however, Danielle had been the first woman he had ever been attracted to. Before that, Trey had always assumed he was attracted only to men. It had been an eye-opener for him . . . and the beginning of the end for Jake and Trey's relationship . . . even though Trey had never acted on that attraction.

"She was very pretty . . . and sweet," Jake said.

A little withdrawn, though. But Trey and Jake had drawn her out of her shell and formed a friendship with her. She didn't make friends easily, but it had been clear she really wanted to connect to people. She just didn't know how. Once she moved away, though, they never heard from her again.

Jake wondered if that was about to change.

Danielle lay in her bed, wishing sleep would come . . . wishing she were in her own bed at home. She hated sleeping in a strange place, especially a hotel room. She'd spent several hours on the computer, finishing her latest game quest with her online friends and getting enough experience points to level up. She'd thought that would tire her out enough to fall right to sleep, but she'd been wrong.

She heard male voices in the hall outside her room. Listening carefully, she could make out Trey's voice. The other was probably Jake's. But earlier this evening when she'd passed by the lounge, she'd noticed the men with a beautiful blonde. Could it be that Jake and Trey were taking the woman to their room?

She rolled her eyes at her own thoughts. She was in the middle of a long sexual dry spell, and it was turning her into a major horn ball.

She pounded her pillow. Rolled back and forth. Looked at the clock again. She drew in a deep breath at the thought of the two men opening their door, inviting the woman in . . . *inviting Danielle in.*

She could toss on a sexy bit of nothing under a robe and slip over to their room . . . knock on the door . . . invite herself in. Her nipples pebbled at the thought.

Well, maybe she could indulge herself a little longer. After all, a little innocent fantasizing never hurt anyone.

TWO

Danielle imagined she was in the room with Trey and Jake. *Jake took her in his arms and kissed her, his masculine lips caressing hers with tenderness, quickly turning to urgency. He stripped off her clothes until she stood naked in front of him. Trey's hands stroked over her breasts from behind.*

Danielle stripped off her loose pajama top, then kicked off the bottoms. Her fingers slipped between her thighs. *Trey's big, warm hands encased her breasts as Jake tossed off his clothing. She gazed at his huge, rigid cock. He pulled her against his hard body and kissed her again while Trey pulled off his clothes. Both men stood in front of her . . . big, masculine, and naked. She grabbed both their cocks and stroked.*

"Do you want me?" she asked.

"Oh, baby, you don't know how much," Trey responded, then kissed her passionately.

Jake lay on the bed and Trey turned her around to face Jake.

She prowled over him, then lowered herself onto Jake's huge, rigid cock. It was big and hard . . . and stretched her as it pushed deep inside.

Danielle's fingers swirled inside her hot opening.

She leaned forward and Trey climbed behind her, then pressed his long rod against her behind. As she squeezed Jake inside her vagina, Trey pushed his cockhead into her back opening.

Her fingers twirled faster. She'd never experienced anal sex, but she wanted to. With Trey and Jake. So she could experience both of them at the same time.

Danielle loved the feel of Jake's cock inside her as Trey pressed his impressive penis into her back opening, filling her full of rock-hard male flesh. Jake began to move, thrusting into her in long even strokes. She moaned softly, thrusting her fingers inside her slick opening. *Jake fucked her hard, driving his cock into her, as Trey glided back and forth in her back opening.*

Danielle arched upward, then slipped over the edge, her insides quivering with pleasure.

She flopped back on the bed, gasping for air. Oh God, she wished she could be with them for real. The two of them pressed against her, giving her pleasure . . . wanting her . . . And the best part . . . well, almost the best part . . . would be lying in Trey's and Jake's arms afterward.

As she lay in her bed, hot and sweaty—and alone— she felt empty. Her immediate need had been sated, but she longed to be lying in a man's arms. Cherished. And loved.

The next morning, Danielle went for a swim in the hotel pool, then took a leisurely stroll before having a late breakfast. She returned to her room and relaxed for a while before showering.

She stood in front of the mirror and dried her hair with the hotel hair dryer. It took quite a while to get the mass of long wavy auburn hair dry. Then she put on her makeup.

Who would be there this evening? Trey and Jake, of course. And it would be nice to see Harmony again, though Danielle knew they'd get very little time to talk, if any, since as the bride, Harmony would be busy talking to all the guests over the evening. A quick hello and a "how are you doing" would probably be about it.

She returned to the bedroom and donned her pink bra and panty set, then her panty hose. As she pulled on her standard aqua party dress, she wondered if she should have bought something new. Different. She swished her long auburn curls over her shoulder, and examined her reflection. Something sexy.

But no one here had seen this dress, and it was perfectly fine, with its lace trim across the top of the bodice and the swishy knee-length skirt. It was great for dancing . . . if anyone asked her to dance.

Like Trey or Jake. At the reception, she might get a chance to dance with them and maybe flirt a little . . . and that could lead to . . .

Nothing. What the heck was wrong with her? They didn't get involved with women.

Still, she'd like to look her best tonight. There would be other men there, too. Ones who *did* like women. And after the hormone rush from last night's fantasies of Trey and Jake, she thought it would be great if she could hook up with someone tonight. A real man rather than an imaginary one.

If only she knew how to do that.

Oh, damn, why didn't I bring something sexy to wear?

Danielle smoothed her skirt, eyeing the simple round neckline and the shape that did nothing to show off her figure, despite the belted waist. She remembered the lovely dress boutique around the corner from the hotel with the stunning black dress in the window.

She glanced at the clock on the bedside table. 2:20 P.M.

Oh well. Nothing I can do about it now.

She ran a brush through her hair one more time, then pulled her light knit wrap around her shoulders and picked up her evening bag. A few minutes later, she stepped from the elevator to the bustling hotel lobby. She walked toward the front door, intending to ask the doorman to find her a cab.

"Well, hello, stranger."

Danielle glanced around at the familiar male voice. There stood Cole Grant, with his black, wavy hair skimming his collar, and a glint in his charcoal gray eyes.

She smiled warmly. "Cole. How nice to see you."

"Is that all I get? How about a hug?"

She opened her arms and hugged him, a little rigid at first, but melting into the warmth of his friendly embrace. She and Cole and Harmony had spent a lot of time together in their first year of college, becoming the closest thing to friends Danielle had ever known. But she had been there only one year before she'd transferred to Northeastern University in Boston, and over ten more years had passed since then. She was surprised that Cole even remembered her.

He grinned, then released her. "You are as gorgeous as ever."

The doorman opened the door as they approached, and she stepped outside into the warm June sunshine, Cole behind her.

"You want to share a cab to the wedding?" asked Cole.

"That would be nice."

Cole gestured to the doorman, and within a few moments a cab pulled up in front of them and Cole opened the door. Danielle slid into the backseat and Cole settled in beside her. He told the driver the name of the church, and then the car pulled into the early-afternoon traffic.

"So it's nice that Harmony's getting married. Have you met the groom?" Danielle asked.

"Yes, I've met Aiden, and he's a great guy. Perfect for her. I'm sure he'll make her very happy."

"And what about you? Is there someone special in your life?"

He stared out the window wistfully. "No, not yet, but

I haven't given up on finding the perfect woman yet. How about you?"

"I don't date women." She grinned and he laughed at her obvious sidestep maneuver.

"And Mr. Right? Is he hanging around back home waiting for your return?"

"If he was, do you think I'd be going to a wedding dateless?"

"Ah, the perpetual search for love. Life never makes it easy."

He'd certainly said a mouthful. Life had never made anything easy for Danielle. Not from the time she'd been dropped off into foster care when she was a toddler. Actually, foster care was a step up from living with her mother . . . a woman with severe emotional problems who simply saw her as a huge inconvenience, and didn't care what happened to her.

Danielle had lived her whole life with the pain of knowing that the one person who should love her no matter what . . . her mother . . . didn't want her. She knew her mother faced a lot of demons—being in and out of mental hospitals and drug rehab facilities for most of her life. Even so, if Danielle couldn't win the love of her own mother, why did she think she'd ever win the love of a man?

The cab pulled up in front of a lovely stone church with a beautiful stained-glass window over its huge arched doors.

Danielle placed her hand on the arm Cole offered as they walked up the steps to the doors, then stepped into the church. The usher led them to a pew on the left side of the aisle, about five rows from the front. The sweet scent of fresh flowers filled the air.

As more people drifted into the church, she glanced around and saw a few faces she vaguely remembered. A few moments later, she saw Jake and Trey arrive. The pew Danielle and Cole sat in had filled up—a young couple with three children—and so had the couple of rows behind them, so Trey and Jake sat several rows back. They didn't notice Danielle as they sat down, both looking exceptionally handsome in their dark, well-tailored suits.

"Ah, there's Trey and Jake," said Cole.

"I saw them checking into the hotel yesterday, but I didn't get a chance to say hello. Have you seen them since college?"

"Oh, I see them from time to time."

"Are they still together?"

Before Cole got a chance to respond, the organ music began, signaling the bride's arrival.

A lovely bridesmaid in a soft violet dress proceeded up the aisle, followed by another, then another, then another. Danielle sighed. They were so beautiful. Their dresses, snug in the bodice, the skirts flowing in a softly draping fabric, flattered their graceful figures, and they carried pretty bouquets of soft pink roses.

19

The organ music paused, then the wedding march began. Harmony glowed as she walked up the aisle, luminous in a beaded, fitted bodice with a sweetheart neckline and a full-length skirt. Her veil flowed to the ground, a light froth over the train that swept along behind her in delicate waves of white beaded satin. She carried a lovely bouquet of roses in soft pink, dark rose, and lavender, interspersed with baby's breath.

As Danielle watched Harmony approach the man waiting for her at the front of the church, her heart swelled at the amazing look of love on the handsome man's face. His brown eyes glowed with warmth as he smiled at her, revealing a charming dimple in his cheek and softening the strong line of his square jaw. He obviously cared deeply for Harmony.

As the ceremony proceeded, and Danielle heard the words of love they shared in their vows to each other, their gazes locked in a look of absolute adoration, a shiver ran through her. Cole handed her a handkerchief to wipe the tears trickling from her eyes. She felt truly honored to be a witness to this joining. Warmth washed through her as she realized, with a deep and unbending confidence, that these two were meant to be together and that their love would last a lifetime.

Harmony had found true love. Something Danielle hadn't even known she believed in . . . until now.

Danielle dabbed at her eyes as Harmony and Aiden turned to face their guests.

"I would like to present, for the first time, Mr. and Mrs. Aiden and Harmony Curtis." The minister beamed as he began the applause.

Harmony and Aiden kissed one more time, then proceeded down the aisle to a swell of organ music, followed by the wedding party. Once they had all left the church, the guests began their orderly exit.

The sun shone brightly as Danielle watched people take pictures of the happy couple, who stood at the top of the stone stairs outside the church. People milled around. Family members, reunited by this happy event, embraced. Children laughed and raced around the lovely park behind the church, happy to be out in the sunshine.

Danielle plucked at her skirt, uncertain whether it was too soon to leave. The reception wasn't for another two hours, so she figured she'd return to the hotel and relax during the downtime.

"Did you bring your camera?"

She glanced up at Cole's voice. "Camera?"

"We could go over and get some pictures of the happy couple."

"Uh, no, I didn't think to bring it. You go ahead," she continued. "I think I'll just go back to the hotel."

She walked toward the parking lot and pulled her cell phone from her small purse to call for a cab.

"Hey, Danielle. Wait."

Danielle turned around at the sound of Harmony's voice. There was the bride, clinging to her full skirt, hurrying down the last few steps. Danielle walked toward her, and Harmony scooped her into a warm embrace, hugging her tight to her body.

"It's been such a long time. I'm glad you could make it." Harmony drew back and smiled brightly. "Thank you so much for coming."

"Well, uh . . . thank you for inviting me."

"I missed you when you left Carleton Falls U. It was never quite the same without you."

"Oh. Thanks." Danielle had always assumed the people she'd become close to there had forgotten about her after she'd left. After all, she had been there only a year. The friendships, if she could even call them that, had been short-lived. She had been quite shocked when she'd received the wedding invitation from Harmony.

And quite pleased. Now this show of affection and genuine pleasure at seeing her touched her heart.

"I . . . uh . . . missed you, too." And she had.

"So how have you been doing?" Harmony asked.

"Well, I . . ."

A couple stepped toward Harmony.

"Oh, hang on, honey. This is my aunt and uncle and they have to leave."

"Of course."

Danielle rearranged her wrap around her shoulders as the couple congratulated Harmony and gave her hugs and kisses. Self-consciously, Danielle clung to her evening bag with both hands as several other people continued the congratulations, kissing Harmony's cheek, shaking her hand, giving her more hugs.

Harmony's friendship had meant a lot to Danielle. It had started when they'd been assigned to share a residence room. Harmony had been intent on drawing out her quiet, introverted roommate. Slowly, Danielle had opened up to Harmony's friendly warmth, and they'd become friends. It had been wonderful to have someone to talk to, whether just to talk about her day or to discuss her problems. Not that she'd done the latter very often.

When her financial situation had forced her to leave Carleton Falls, in favor of Northeastern University's co-op program, Harmony had tried to keep in touch, but Danielle had let the friendship fizzle out, probably because she'd believed they'd only drift apart anyway.

"Now, Dani, you were saying."

A couple more people came up and stood beside Danielle, waiting to talk to the bride.

"Darn, we're not going to get a chance to talk here. You are still coming to the reception, right?"

"Of course," Danielle answered, though she wished she could just leave shortly after dinner. She wasn't good at these social things.

"Good. I've put you at the table with Trey and Jake." Harmony winked.

Danielle's heart skipped a beat. Back at college, Danielle had confided in Harmony about her attraction to the two men, and her frustration. She had forgotten how much she had opened up to Harmony back then.

"Are they still a couple?" Danielle asked.

"No, afraid not. But . . ." Harmony leaned in close to Danielle's ear. "You know they date women now?"

"Really?" Shock rippled through her . . . followed by a surge of joy.

Harmony leaned in close again. "You know, tonight would be a good time to pursue that one particular fantasy of yours."

Danielle's eyes widened, her cheeks burning.

Harmony laughed. "Don't tell me you forgot you told me about that. Of course, it was after a pitcher of beer in the pub, and it took a lot of cajoling from me, but you know, there's nothing wrong with a little casual sex. Especially between old friends." She winked. "Believe me, I'm sure it'll be an experience you'll never forget."

"You think . . . they might . . . consider it?" Danielle's

hand covered her traitorous mouth. She couldn't believe she'd uttered those words out loud.

Harmony giggled. "I'm *sure* they would." She hugged Danielle tightly. "Honey, don't let this opportunity slip away." Her voice had turned serious. "Everyone should grab their dream when they have the chance. No matter how wild or crazy."

Danielle sat in the cab heading to the hotel, watching the buildings pass by.

Harmony had placed her at a table with Trey and Jake. Her heart quivered. The two men she had fantasized about for years were finally available. They liked women, and they weren't attached.

She actually had a chance with them. But she had only this one night.

Should she take advantage of it?

Harmony's words echoed through her brain.

Don't let this opportunity slip away. Everyone should grab their dream when they have the chance. No matter how wild or crazy.

She glanced down at her aqua dress and shook her head. An image of the spectacular, and quite sexy, black gown she'd admired in the little shop window this morning sprang into mind.

Maybe she'd make a little stop on the way back to her room.

Three

Danielle stepped toward the reception hall feeling a little conspicuous. This was not the sort of dress she usually wore. She stopped in front of a mirror in the hallway just outside the atrium and checked the neckline. The black dress hugged her breasts, accentuating the way her new bra pressed them up and forward. The bodice was a halter style, revealing a lot of cleavage. Cleavage she didn't normally have without the help of the black lace underwired push-up bra she'd bought along with the dress . . . and the black lace garter belt with little red satin bows . . . and black stockings. And a matching thong. *She never wore a thong.*

She also wore long black gloves, which made her feel ultra sexy. And shoes with heels so high she suspected that if she fell, she'd probably break her neck. But they made her legs look long and sexy. Not that anyone would see that with the long skirt, but if she was successful tonight . . .

So maybe the shoes did pinch, and the bra squeezed a mite too much . . . not to mention the way the thong pulled into her butt. But it would all be worth it . . . if her fantasy came true.

She pushed back her shoulders and took a step forward, concentrating on remaining tall and steady on these stiltlike shoes. It was time to pursue a dream.

"Wow."

Trey glanced in the direction of Jake's stare.

"Wow is right. Isn't that Danielle Rayne?" Trey said.

"That's right." Cole also watched the tall, incredibly built woman with the flowing auburn curls approach their table. "But I sat with her at the wedding, and that's not what she was wearing then."

"Looks like we're in luck." Jake glanced at the empty chair beside Trey. "I think she's our missing guest."

Salad had already been served and they had thought the eighth guest at the table had been a no-show.

As Danielle approached the table, Cole stood up. "Danielle. I thought you'd gotten lost," he said as he pulled the chair out for her.

"I . . . had a few things I had to do. I didn't mean to be so late."

He smiled. "Well, you were certainly worth the wait."

Her cheeks flushed as she sat down.

"Danielle, you remember Trey and Jake?"

Danielle's gaze fell on Jake, then shifted to Trey. "Of course."

Trey smiled. He remembered Danielle well. She'd been very quiet and withdrawn when she'd first arrived at Carleton Falls. Not at all like the woman sitting beside him now. But Harmony had drawn her out. The two women had befriended Trey and Jake and they'd formed a close friendship which had, unfortunately, lasted only a year. That's when Danielle had transferred to school in Boston, where she went into a co-op program. She had no family—at least none who acknowledged her—so the extra money had been a godsend for her.

Trey had always liked Danielle . . . a lot.

He'd often wondered what it would be like to make love to Danielle. She'd always had a sultry, subtle sensuality about her. In that dress, which he could tell by the way she periodically tugged at the neckline was not her usual style, she oozed raw sexual intensity. She'd worn that dress for a reason tonight. The question was, what reason?

She'd sat with Cole at the wedding. Had she decided to pursue him?

She took a bite of her salad, and then her tongue glided over her glossy red lips in a delicate caress. His groin tightened. Man, he couldn't help wishing it was him she wanted.

Trey took a sip of wine as the waiter placed a plate of prime rib in front of him.

"So, Trey, what did you wind up majoring in?" Danielle picked up her knife and fork and speared a glazed carrot from her plate.

"Computers."

She took a bite of the carrot, and he couldn't help watching her delicious-looking glossy lips as she chewed.

Jake grabbed a roll from the basket in front of him. "He loves gadgets. You should see his place. High-tech devices galore."

Trey dipped a chunk of his succulent beef in the small bowl of au jus on his plate, then took a bite.

She leaned her chin on her hand and smiled at Trey. "Like what?"

Trey shrugged. Women didn't care about stuff like that.

"He has one of those robot vacuums," Jake said.

"Oh, that's right." Cole chuckled. "He has a great video of his cat riding around on it."

"Your cat rides the vacuum?" She stared at him in wide-eyed fascination. "I thought cats hated vacuums."

"Not mine. Hickory thinks it's his own personal toy."

"You'll have to show me the video sometime." She smiled, then glanced down shyly when his gaze met hers. When she glanced up again, he almost expected her to flutter her eyelashes.

He grinned. Well, damn, the woman was flirting with him.

As dinner progressed, Trey found himself becoming confused. Although Danielle seemed to be paying him a lot of attention, she paid an equal amount of attention to Jake. Maybe he had misread the situation and she just wanted to catch up with old friends. She'd never been really comfortable interacting with the opposite sex. Back in the old days, he and Jake had sometimes offered her advice when she was interested in one guy or another . . . or if one was bothering her because she was sending the wrong signals.

Maybe that was the problem now. She certainly was sending out strong signals that she was interested, but maybe she didn't intend to.

Once the waiter cleared away the dessert plates and re-filled the coffee cups, Danielle excused herself to go to the ladies' room.

Trey turned to Jake.

"Do you get what's going on with Danielle?" Jake asked before Trey had a chance to speak.

Harmony stepped up behind Jake and placed her arm around his shoulder affectionately. "I'll tell you." She leaned in close so only the two of them could hear. "Danielle is interested in you."

"Who?" Trey asked at the same time as Jake.

"*Both* of you." She leaned her veiled head in close between them, resting a hand on Trey's shoulder. "Look, I probably shouldn't be telling you this, but"—she glanced in the direction of the door, then back to them—"I'm sure it will help things along. Danielle has always had a crush on you guys, but you were in a relationship together, so she thought it was impossible."

"So she's happy to be with either one of us?" Jake asked.

"Well, that would work, but . . ." Harmony grinned impishly. "I think she'd be willing . . . well, more than willing to . . ." She paused, her eyes glittering. Discreetly, she glanced around again.

Heat wafted through Trey as her implication hit him. "You're telling us she wants a threesome? With us?" he asked. "Shy Danielle?"

The thought of making love to sweet Danielle . . . and with Jake . . . sent heat flooding to his groin.

"Yes, she is shy," Harmony continued. "And she's not used to doing this. But she knows you two . . . you used to be friends after all . . . and she's always wanted to hook up with you guys. I suggested that tonight might be her chance." Her hand gently tightened on Trey's shoulder. "You guys aren't going to let her down, are you?"

Danielle clinked her glass with the others at yet another toast to the bride and groom, Harmony gazing happily into Aiden's eyes.

She glanced toward Trey. Jake's hand rested on Trey's arm as he leaned in to say something. Trey laughed, his brown eyes glittering. She could see the affection in Jake's

31

warm blue eyes, and the easy camaraderie between the two men. Maybe it was just her take on things, but she definitely felt they still cared about each other, even if it was only as close friends.

What had happened between them? Why weren't they still together?

The music started and the happy couple proceeded to the dance floor for the first dance. Soon the bridal party joined them, and everyone watched as the couples swirled around the floor to the rhythm of the music.

"Danielle, would you like to dance?"

Goose bumps quivered along her neck as Trey stood up and held out his hand to her.

She nodded and stood up. He led her to the glossy wooden dance floor. When his arms slid around her, ripples of warmth wafted through her. Light glinted off his diamond earring as he smiled at her, and she longed to run her fingers through his tousled, sandy-colored hair. As they moved to the music, the heat of his hand on her lower back and his other hand enveloping hers, guiding her with such masterful expertise, sent her senses swirling.

He was a wonderful dancer. Smooth. With a stylish flair. She felt light and sure of herself under his capable lead.

The song ended and the music changed to a strong, vibrant beat.

"Do you know how to tango?" He did not release her.

"No, not really."

His right hand slid around her to rest under her shoulder blade, drawing her body close to his, and he extended his left arm outward to just above her shoulder. Her breasts pressed tight against him and she could feel his incredible heat as the music surged through them.

For a moment, he simply held her in this intimate stance, their bodies tall and straight, yet intensely, sensually close.

"This is Argentine tango," he murmured in her ear, "so you'll step forward with your left foot, take one step to the right, then move back four steps. Okay?"

She nodded.

"On the third step back, you'll cross your left foot in front of your right. After your last step back, you'll step left, then feet together."

She shook her head. "I . . . don't quite get it."

He smiled, pressing his arm more snugly around her. "You will."

At his first step, drawing her forward with his hand on her back, she could tell she was in good hands. He stepped to the side, then pressed her backward. One step. Two.

"Now cross, then back."

Instead of moving her left foot back, she crossed it in front of her right foot, as he instructed, then moved her right foot back. Then he glided her left and forward, where her feet magically wound up together, just as he'd said.

"That's the basic step. We'll do that a few times, to get used to it."

He led her around the floor, reminding her of the crossover, until it became second nature and they moved in a fluid motion.

Soon she forgot about her feet, overwhelmed by the heat of his body and the sensual beat pulsing through her.

"You've definitely got it. Now let's try something new."

"No, I don't think so."

But suddenly he spun her around several times, then she found her back pressed against his front, his arm under her breasts. Her body flowed with his, her feet obeying as they moved across the floor. As the music slowed, his hand glided to her neck. His fingers curled around her jaw, and he turned her to face him again. Their gazes locked. His arm firmly around her waist, he dipped her backward, his lips moving closer to hers until they were a whisper's breath away. They froze for a breathless second . . . then he drew her up and into his arms. The beat accelerated. With their flurry of movement around the dance floor and the heat of their bodies mingling, she found it hard to catch her breath. As the music slowed again, he spun her away to one side, then the other, then drew her back, into a deep dip. Their gazes locked in a sizzling exchange as he drew her up again. His hand cupped her head and he drew her face closer to his. Closer. She longed for his lips to capture hers. For his tongue to plunder her mouth in a searing invasion.

34

The music ended. She sucked in a breath.

So close.

He relaxed his hold and eased away.

"Thank you. That was . . . wonderful." She'd felt vibrant and sexy on the dance floor. Because of Trey.

He smiled. "Any time."

"May I cut in?" Jake stepped beside Trey.

"Of course." Trey kissed her hand, then smiled warmly at Jake before he headed back to the table.

Jake smiled at her, his dark blue eyes twinkling in the dim light, as he drew her close, his arm encircling her waist. He swept her around the floor to the music.

She liked how he'd grown his light brown hair long enough that he wore it tied neatly behind his head in a short ponytail, and she longed to reach back and release it, then drag her fingers through it.

"It's been a long time since we were together at college. How has life been treating you?" he asked.

"Not bad," she said, relieved he wasn't going to twirl her into another exotic dance. As much as she'd enjoyed doing the tango with Trey, she didn't think her senses could handle another. "I wish I'd been able to continue at Carleton Falls, though. I really missed all of you."

He drew her closer to the heat of his body. "And we missed you."

His warm gaze held her mesmerized. He'd always been so warm and friendly toward her. Always been there if she'd needed to talk. Not that she'd opened up much, but it had been nice knowing he was there if she'd wanted to.

The feel of his sturdy arms around her . . . his heart beating against hers . . . his face so close she could easily lift her lips to his in an exhilarating kiss . . . sent her into a sensual swirl.

Longing washed through her . . . to fulfill her heart's desire. To be wanted and loved. To really connect with someone. If only for a single night.

She had always wanted to be with Jake and Trey . . . ever since she'd first met them. Their sensitivity, their compassionate natures, their obvious capacity for love . . . Those things had attracted her right from the beginning. And had been why she'd felt they would be together as a couple forever. She couldn't interfere with a love like that.

Yet, they weren't together now. So, not only would being with her *not* come between them, but in this case, it would bring them together . . . at least for one night.

As she gazed into Jake's midnight eyes, she knew he could give her what she wanted. She trusted Jake. And Trey.

And that trust gave her strength.

The closeness of his body triggered images from her steamy dreams of him and Trey, sending her senses into turmoil. The memory of her fantasy last night mingled with her dream memories and she felt a deep yearning to live out her long-term fantasy to be with both of them.

She wanted him. And she wanted Trey. Tonight. But how could she possibly suggest . . . ?

The song ended. He gazed down at her.

"How about we get a drink?"

She nodded. He took her hand and they walked across the dance floor toward the bar. Before they reached the line of people waiting for drinks, Trey approached holding a beer in one hand and a creamy red cocktail in a tulip glass in the other.

"I think I know exactly what you'd like." Trey grinned and held out the stemmed glass. "A Ménage à Trois."

Her heart seemed to stop. She blinked at him . . . then realized he meant the drink.

She didn't care. This was her opening. It was now or never.

"You're right. That's exactly what I want." She reached out and took the glass from his hand. "And I'd like this, too." She took a sip, then tugged Jake's hand. "Let's go."

Four

Danielle finished the drink as they walked along the atrium, then abandoned the empty glass on a side table. Jake walked ahead and pushed the call button for the elevator. The doors whooshed open and they stepped inside. Trey pushed the button labeled 15 and the doors slid closed.

Danielle said nothing as the elevator rose, tensing as she realized she was in it now. No backing out.

Not that she wanted to, but . . . what did they think of her?

They're men. They think it's great.

The door opened and she stepped out. As they strolled down the hall, she said, "Let's go to my room."

She pushed her key card into the slot and opened the door. They stepped inside, and suddenly the room that had seemed quite spacious felt far too small with these two tall, broad-shouldered men filling it.

"Uh . . . should I order something from room service?" she asked. "Some drinks?"

Jake stepped toward her. "We don't need any drinks."

"And . . . uh . . . what about . . . protection?" she asked. "I mean, I'm on the pill, but . . ."

"I've been tested recently," said Jake.

"Me, too. No worries here." Trey grinned.

"I haven't been with anyone since I was last tested." She didn't want to mention that had been over a year ago.

Jake's hands slid around her waist and he drew her close. His lips grazed the side of her neck and she gasped at the heat that careened through her. She stepped back, only to bump into Trey, who stood behind her and began to kiss the other side of her neck. Jake stepped forward again and she found herself sandwiched between the two of them. Their lips danced along the sides of her neck, sending quivers rippling through her. The sexual energy of their three bodies collided in an explosive intensity. She grasped Jake's shoulders, needing the stability.

Trey's hands encircled her waist and he turned her around to face him. His lips captured hers. She melted against him as his tongue pressed between her lips and stroked inside. She ran her fingers through his short, sun-streaked hair. As his tongue tangled with hers, Jake's hands stroked over her breasts and caressed her with a gentle pressure.

She felt the zipper of her dress glide downward, then

the two buttons at the back of her neck unfasten. Her dress dropped to her waist, revealing her breasts clad in the lacy black bra. Trey drew her forward as he backed up, like he had on the dance floor. When he reached the bed, he sat down and stared at her breasts with frank male appreciation.

Oh God, she never thought she'd be here, like this. It was the craziest thing she'd ever done. And she was loving every minute of it.

Jake's hands covered her breasts, then Trey's hands covered Jake's and both men caressed her.

Jake stroked down her ribs, then eased her dress over her hips and let it fall to the floor. His hands stroked over her bare bottom. One on each round expanse of flesh. Stroking. Driving her wild. He nuzzled her neck, then nibbled her ear.

As Trey stroked his fingers over the swell of her breasts, over the lacy cups, Jake released the hooks on the back of her bra. Trey drew it forward and tossed it aside. At the feel of the cool air, her nipples jutted forward.

"You have beautiful breasts," Trey said.

Jake's hands cupped them, then his fingertips stroked over her hard nipples. She dropped her head back, resting it against Jake's shoulder. Trey leaned forward and captured one nipple in his mouth. She moaned at the pure, blissful sensation of his hot mouth on her hard nub. Licking . . . tugging . . . sucking it deep inside.

Trey turned her around and kissed her back as Jake

captured her dry nipple in his mouth, leaving the other one cold and needy. She stroked Jake's head, then reached behind and unfastened the leather tie to release his long hair, then ran her fingers through it. Trey's hand stroked over her behind, and she felt him tug on the elastic waistband of her thong and roll it downward. It glided down her thighs, past her calves to her ankles.

"Those are pretty high heels you have there," he said as he tugged the panties over the long spikes. She lifted one foot, then the other as he freed the thong, then tossed it aside.

"They make your legs look incredible," Jake said.

She started to remove her long black gloves, but Jake stopped her.

"Leave them on. They're incredibly sexy, especially with the garter belt and stockings."

"And nothing else," Trey said, his cinnamon brown eyes glittering.

She caught her reflection in the dresser mirror—her breasts naked, her auburn curls framed by the garter belt and dark stockings—and she had to admit the image was pretty hot. Especially since she stood between two handsome hunks still fully clothed . . . in tailored suits.

"Okay, now you two."

She sat on the bed and watched as the two of them shrugged off their jackets and loosened their ties. Jake tugged the loop of his unfastened tie over his head and tossed it away, while Trey patiently untied the knot on his. Jake unfastened a couple of buttons on his shirt, then tugged it over his head, revealing taut, well-maintained muscles across his chest and shoulders. Hot and hard man flesh. Goose bumps quivered across her arms. Jake's pants fell to the floor as Trey unbuttoned his shirt. As it fell open, Danielle caught sight of the tight six-pack abs under the shirt, then the tight, incredibly well-sculpted muscles of his arms and chest.

She licked her lips.

The two men now stood before her in just their underwear. Jake was a briefs man, and Trey wore boxers.

"Oh, you both look incredible."

She wanted to savor the moment. To just look at them, the bulges pushing at the light cotton of their underwear telling her they wanted her. Almost as much as she wanted them. And had wanted them for what seemed like forever.

But now, with the moment upon her, she wasn't sure. . . . How could she do this?

How ridiculous? Here she sat, basically naked, except for accessories . . . and she was having second thoughts?

She had wanted this forever.

But wanting something and making it a reality were two very different things.

"You know, I think our girl is having second thoughts," Jake said to Trey.

He stepped toward her and knelt in front of her. Trey sat beside her on the bed. The heat of these two hot, virile men so close sent her senses reeling.

Jake took her hand and kissed the back of it, his lips playing along her knuckles in a gentle caress. "You know, Danielle, you were a very special friend to us. You accepted Trey and me without a second thought even though our relationship was unconventional. You were sweet and giving."

Trey took her other hand and squeezed it gently. "Not to mention gorgeous. It's hard not to feel attraction to a woman who looks like you do."

"This isn't just a one-night stand," said Jake. "This is the culmination of years of a building attraction that all three of us want to explore."

All three of us. This was more than just her with two men. This was Jake and Trey sharing sexual intimacy, too. For whatever reason they had broken up, they clearly still liked being together. . . . She sensed the easy warmth and comfort they shared. Maybe this need to share a woman was more than just the typical male fantasy. Maybe it was a way for them to share intimacy with each other.

Trey cupped her cheek with his strong hand and she leaned against it, closing her eyes as Jake stroked her hair back from her face.

"Even when Jake and I were together, we used to wonder what it would be like to be with you."

She opened her eyes. "Really? So even then . . . you were attracted to women?"

Jake nuzzled behind her ear. "We're not talking about any woman. We're talking about you."

She didn't know if it was true, or if they were just flattering her, but her heart swelled at the words. Just the fact that they'd say such things to put her at ease showed that they were sensitive and giving.

She smiled and stood up. "Well, if you've wanted me for all those years . . ." She cupped her hands under her breasts and lifted them, stroking her tight nipples with her thumbs. "Let's make this spectacular."

Jake shifted to the bed, sitting beside Trey. They both watched her thumbs circle around and around, their eyes darkening in desire. She slid one hand down her ribs, over the lacy garter belt, then dipped past the curls into the slick flesh below.

"I'm really turned on." She sauntered toward them and knelt down, then placed one hand on each of their bulges. "Mmm. You're both so big. And hard."

She slipped her hand inside Jake's briefs, thrilling at the silky feel of the skin stretched over his rock-hard cock. And the heat! She wrapped her hand around him and drew out his searing cock. It popped upward. She marveled at its considerable length as she stroked up and down.

"Lovely." She turned to Trey, who was watching her hand firmly around Jake, still stroking. "Now yours."

She slipped her hand inside his boxers and found his thick cock. She drew it out, in wonder at the feel of two hot hard cocks in her hands. Trey's wasn't as long as Jake's, but it was thicker and curved upward in a delightful manner.

She stroked both of them, up and down, in rhythm.

"You both have such big sexy cocks." She didn't usually use language like that, but she didn't usually have sex with two men, either. It was a night to act a little out of character.

She leaned forward and kissed the tip of Trey's red-faced erection. Then she leaned toward Jake's purple-tinged member and kissed it, too. Then she wrapped her lips around Jake and sucked in his cockhead.

She stroked around it with her tongue, swirling around and back several times, to his appreciative murmurs. Then she released him and leaned over to Trey's. His cockhead filled her mouth a little more and she stroked over the tip with her tongue, then sucked on him. She sucked him deeper, moving down his shaft, then returned to Jake and swallowed him deep into her mouth. Her hand still stroked Trey, up and down.

She leaned back. "You know, I think this would work better if you two moved closer together."

Jake shifted against Trey, their thighs pressing together. She tugged on their cocks a little, pushing the heads together. Jake's eyes darkened to a deep navy blue and Trey's glimmered with heat. She began to lick the tip of Jake's cock, then Trey's, then back and forth from one to the other. She swirled her tongue around the lower edge of one cockhead, then the other, laving the hot male flesh. Back and forth. She opened her mouth and took Trey inside, then opened wider and pressed Jake in, too. Jake groaned. Both cockheads filled her mouth. Both men moaned as she squeezed and sucked on them. She pushed her mouth down as far as she could, taking as much of their shafts as her mouth would allow. Her hands stroked up and down each of them, then glided lower and cupped their balls. She massaged them gently as she alternated sucking and licking their cocks.

Jake groaned.

"Danielle," Trey murmured. "That is . . . Ohhh."

He tensed and his cock pulsed in her mouth, followed immediately by Jake, filling her mouth with hot liquid. She continued pumping and sucking.

Both men flopped back on the bed, spent. Trey's arm sprawled across Jake's sculpted chest while Jake's hand rested on Trey's thigh.

She stood up and stroked her hard, needy nipples as she watched them with a smile. Trey pushed himself to his feet and stepped behind her.

"Let me help you with those." He cupped her breasts and gently caressed; then his fingers captured one nipple and he toyed with it while Jake stepped toward her and took her other nipple into his hot, wet mouth.

She moaned at the gentle torment of his tongue flicking over her hard nub. Trey's hands strayed lower until he stroked over her curls, gently caressing them at first, then slipping his fingers along her damp folds and then into her tight, wet opening.

"Jake, she's really ready for us."

Jake glanced down at his already reviving member. "And I'm about ready for her."

She reached around behind her and stroked down Trey's stomach until she reached his cock. To her surprise, it was already hard again, too.

"You're both so enthusiastic."

Trey nuzzled her neck, sending quivers through her body.

"You bet we are, sexy."

The words made her feel special and wanted. Hot desire shot through her. She needed to express how much she wanted them.

"I want you both to . . . fuck me."

Trey turned her around and captured her mouth with passion.

"And we want to fuck you, sweetheart, but you deserve a little more attention first."

He eased her to the bed and Jake took her arm and drew her back until she was lying down. Jake lapped at one of her nipples and Trey sat down by her other side and licked the other nipple. Suddenly, they were both sucking and she was gasping for air. Trey's hand trailed down her stomach, followed by Jake's, and they both slipped into her wet opening. Two fingers each, stroking inside her.

She moaned. Jake left her nipple and slid down the bed. Then his mouth covered her clit and she gasped. He flicked and cajoled her tight little button until she could barely suck in enough air. Trey leaned in and licked her, too. She could feel their tongues touching each other. Touching her.

Pleasure flooded through her, growing in intensity until she was sure she was going to . . .

They drew away. Jake tugged her downward on the bed until her legs draped over the edge. He knelt at the end of the bed and Trey joined him. Jake pressed his cockhead to her opening and slowly eased it inside her. He continued easing forward until he filled her to the hilt . . . then he drew back. When his cock pulled free she almost sighed in disappointment, but then Trey's cock nudged her opening and he glided inside, stretching her a little more than Jake's more slender cock. He pushed all the way in, then drew back. Jake immediately entered her again. Then Trey. They alternated a few more times, and when Trey was inside her, he wrapped his arms around her and drew her against his body, then tucked her legs around his waist. With his thick cock fully immersed in her, he stood up, cradling her close to his body. She wrapped her arms snugly around him.

Jake moved up behind her. He stroked her thigh, then

over her buttocks . . . then between. She felt a warm moistness as he rubbed her back opening. He was using her moistness as a lubricant. He slid a slick finger inside, then stroked inside her. Then he slid in another finger and stroked and stretched a little. Trey's cock twitched inside her vagina. Oh God, she was so ready for this. She wanted to squirm back against Jake, to feel his long cock slip inside her.

Jake whispered some instructions in her ear, something about pushing her muscles against him, then his slick cock nudged her small opening and pushed in a little. Slowly, he eased in farther . . . then farther . . . until his whole cockhead was inside.

"How you doing, honey?" Jake asked.

She nodded, barely able to stop from screaming that they fuck her now. And hard.

"More," she managed to say.

He grinned and eased forward, his long shaft pushing deeper into her. Finally, he stopped and neither man moved. She was sandwiched between these two muscular men, their rigid cocks deep inside her . . . filling her so full she thought she'd burst with pleasure.

She moaned. "Oh, please fuck me now."

They both chuckled.

Trey drew back, then thrust his cock inside her vagina. Jake began to move, gliding in short strokes in her ass. The two found a rhythm that left her breathless. Stroking her insides with the most exquisite pleasure she'd ever experienced. Hard male flesh. Against her. Inside her. Slick. Moving. Pulsing.

The pleasure spiked.

"Oh God, I'm going to . . ."

Waves of intense sensation swelled through her, crackling across her nerve endings. She gasped. They moved faster. Thrusting. Their slick cocks gliding inside her. She moaned, long and loud, as she seemed to explode in blissful abandon, barely hearing the groan of first one man, then the other as they joined her.

As the last trails of ecstasy wafted away, she rested her head on Trey's shoulder, loving the feel of the two men pressed tight against her.

"That was intense. And wonderful." She kissed Trey's slightly raspy cheek.

Jake drew away, his cock pulling free. She eased her feet to the floor and slid free of Trey's cock. She kissed him lightly on the chin.

"Thank you." She turned to Jake and smiled. "You, too."

"Hmm, it sounds like the lady's ready to get rid of us," Jake said, a glint in his eye.

"Well, no, it's just that . . ."

She figured they had done the wonderful deed, and now they'd want to be heading back to their rooms.

Trey's hand rested on her shoulder and she turned back to him.

"Do you want us to go, Danielle?"

"No, I . . ." It wasn't that she wanted them to go. She just assumed they'd want to.

"Because we'd love to stay," Jake said, stroking her back.

Trey drew her into his arms and kissed her, his lips moving on hers with gentle passion. Jake turned her around and captured her lips with his own insistent persuasion. He released her mouth and gazed into her eyes while Trey nuzzled the nape of her neck.

"I would . . . mmm . . ." Quivers rippled down her spine. ". . . love you to stay."

Jake grinned, and a moment later she found herself lying in bed, a man on each side of her. They stroked and caressed her body with their big hands. Her breasts tingled. Her skin burst into goose bumps. Her thighs parted as one hand stroked over her mound. Trey prowled over her and pressed his cock to her opening, then thrust inside. Jake suckled her nipple while Trey thrust repeatedly into her, sending her hormones soaring. Faster and deeper until her vagina fluttered around him in sensual pulses.

An orgasm swept over her in a mind-numbing wave. Trey groaned and thrust again, erupting inside her. When he pulled free, Jake immediately settled over her and filled her. To her total amazement, as he thrust, another orgasm shuddered through her. Jake pounded deep into her, seeming to sense she wanted it hard and fast. She clung to him and wailed in ecstasy. He groaned and exploded inside her.

When he slid aside, the two of them cradled her between them. She felt warm and protected with these two wonderful men beside her. It was a marvelous feeling.

Five

Danielle awoke with a warm cozy feeling, almost as if she were . . .

She shifted her hand and it bumped against warm flesh. She stroked sideways. Flesh stretched across hard muscle. Opening her eyes, she leaned back a little . . . and came in contact with another male body.

As she blinked at Trey's face, his eyes still closed, she realized she was sandwiched between him and Jake. Last night's fantasy had been very real.

She stroked down Trey's wonderfully tight abs. When her fingers trailed over his pubic curls, she found a swelling cock.

He opened his eyes and smiled. "Looking for something?"

She smiled back as she wrapped her fingers around his rising cock. "Mmm. I think I've found it."

"There's another back here if you want it," Jake said, his hand gliding over her hip.

She didn't think she'd ever stop wanting it. She reached around behind her and captured his long, hard member.

A hard cock in each hand. What a way to start the day.

As she stroked them, Trey leaned down and began to feast on her breast. Jake kissed her neck, then nuzzled and stroked her back, then downward. His hand stroked over her buttocks, around and around while his lips teased her earlobe. He blew little puffs of air in her ear and she sucked in a breath at the lovely sensation.

Oh God, she wanted to spend all morning in bed with them. She wanted each of them to fuck her, then both of them, then more and more and more. Right now she wanted one of them inside her to fill the deep yearning gnawing at her.

She tugged lightly on Trey's cock. He was in the best position right now, his chest against hers, his erection pressed against her mound.

"Trey, I want—"

The warbling sound of the phone ringing interrupted her. It rang again and Jake leaned back, then handed her the receiver.

"Hello?"

An automated voice informed her it was 8:30 A.M. and this was her wake-up call. Oh, damn, she had to catch her flight at 11:30 A.M. She still had to pack and get breakfast and . . . She handed the phone back to Jake.

"I have to get up. My flight . . ."

Trey cupped her breast and lifted, then sucked lightly on her nipple. "Jake and I are already up." He nuzzled her neck. "Do you have to go right this second?"

"Well, I . . ." She glanced at the clock. She did have three hours. If she got dressed fast, and just threw her stuff in the suitcase . . . "Maybe if I skip breakfast."

Jake stroked her back and kissed her ear. "It's an over-rated meal anyway."

She tugged on Trey's cock. "I'm ready now. How about we get the ball rolling?"

Her cheeks flushed as her fingertips brushed his balls. She hadn't intended the pun.

Jake's fingers slipped between her legs and stroked inside her. "She's definitely ready." He moved and she rolled onto her back. Trey climbed over her, and his cockhead nudged her slick opening.

She wrapped her arms around his neck. She felt like fast and furious right now.

"Do it hard and fast, Trey."

He grinned. "My pleasure."

He thrust forward, impaling her with his hard broad cock.

"Ohhh," she moaned.

He stretched her and filled her. She squeezed him, wanting to pull him even deeper inside.

He drew back and thrust forward again.

"Yes, oh, Trey, yes."

He thrust again and again. Pleasure swept through her. She wrapped her legs around his and arched forward, taking him in even deeper.

Jake stroked her breasts as he watched Trey's cock drive into her. Jake leaned forward, his hair brushing across her ribs, and sucked on her nipple, sending electrical sensations rampaging through her as she shot off to heaven. Every cell exploded in a burst of ecstasy.

Trey thrust, then held her tight to his body as he erupted inside her. He kissed her lightly on the mouth, then drew out of her body.

"Ready for more, sweetheart?" Jake asked.

She smiled up at him and just nodded. His cock slipped inside her, reaching deeper than Trey's, and then he began to thrust. Not as fast as Trey, and he did a little spiral thing that caressed her vagina in a wonderfully tantalizing way. He pushed into her, picking up speed until he was like a jackhammer filling her with speed and determination. Suddenly, she shot off the deep end again, blissfully exploding into another intense orgasm.

As she clung to him, she wondered how she'd be able to return to her life without Trey and Jake. She felt so special in their arms—what woman wouldn't?—and being with them like this had been a dream of hers for so long. How could she just walk away?

Danielle glanced around the room—her gaze taking in the clothes strewn around the floor—with a look of panic on her face.

"You go take your shower. Don't worry about this," Trey said.

Fifteen minutes later, when she stepped from the bath-room, tying the terry robe around her waist, she found her suitcase zipped and placed by the front door. Her carry-on sat on the luggage stand, neatly packed but open.

"I assume you have some things in the bathroom to add," Trey said as he saw her glance at the case.

She nodded, amazed at what the men had accomplished in such a short time. Trey wore his shirt and pants, and his jacket and tie were laid neatly across the back of the desk chair. Jake, and his clothes, seemed to be gone.

"Where's Jake?"

"He's gone back to his room to shower. Jake and I catch a flight at eleven thirty and we were wondering if you'd like to share a cab. When does your flight leave?"

She glanced at him. "Mine leaves at eleven thirty, too. I never asked where you're living now."

"Jake and I both live in Carleton Falls."

Which meant they'd be flying to Albany, which was about thirty minutes from Carleton Falls. Her stomach quivered and she sat down on the bed.

"How about you?" Trey asked.

"I live in Phoenicia."

Which meant they were on the same flight.

It also meant seeing Trey and Jake again was not out of the question.

Unless, of course, this was just a one-night thing for them and they didn't want to see her again. Her stomach fluttered again, and for the life of her, she couldn't decide if what she felt was disappointment or relief.

Danielle took another bite of her croissant, smeared liberally with strawberry jam.

"I can't believe you live so close to us and we didn't know it." Jake sipped his coffee.

The three of them had checked out of the hotel and headed to the airport as soon as they were all showered and ready, allowing them enough time to get breakfast at one of the restaurants at the airport.

"I didn't think you'd both still be in Carleton Falls."

Ever since Trey had told her both he and Jake lived in Carleton Falls, Danielle had found herself wondering why they had ever broken up, and if someday they would get back together again. She could still sense a closeness between them that she believed went deeper than mere friendship. She was tempted to ask, but she didn't want to make them feel awkward.

"Carleton Falls is a nice place to live," said Jake. "Trey rides his bike to work every day he can, which is basically from April through December."

"You make it sound like that's a bad thing." Trey pointed his toast at him.

"No, definitely not a bad thing." Jake gazed at Trey's chest and Danielle followed suit, remembering the feel of those tight hard well-defined abs under her fingertips.

No, definitely not bad at all. No wonder Trey was so fit.

"I wish you'd kept in touch," Trey said. "Then maybe we could have gotten together before this."

Danielle swallowed a sip of her tea, guilt niggling through her.

"It was so busy after I transferred, then I had all the extra TA work. . . ." She shrugged, but she knew those were just excuses. The real reason was that she'd assumed they'd all forget about her once she was gone.

"Well, now that we are in touch again, maybe you can come and visit sometime." Trey grinned. "Maybe check out the university for nostalgia's sake."

She nodded. "Sure, that would be great."

Did he really want her to visit, or was he just being polite? She sipped her black currant tea.

A voice over the speaker system announced that their flight would be boarding shortly, so they finished up their breakfast and headed for the gate. As they approached the desk to check in, Danielle slowed a bit.

"What's wrong, Danielle?" Jake asked.

"We won't be sitting together on the flight so . . . I guess this is good-bye."

"Forget about that." Jake plucked the ticket from her hand and stepped up to the desk.

A few moments later, he turned around and handed both her and Trey a boarding pass. They were in adjacent seats.

She grinned broadly. *They want to spend more time with me.*

Boarding began and the three of them walked down the tunnel to the aircraft, then down the aisle of the plane.

"If you'd like the window seat, you can have it," Trey said as he stood in the aisle waiting for her to sit down.

She smiled. "Actually, I think I'd rather sit in the middle."

Trey slid over to the window seat. Jake took her bag and put it in the overhead compartment as she settled in beside Trey. They chatted as passengers continued to board the plane. Once everyone was seated, Jake stood up and grabbed a pillow and blanket from one of the overhead compartments, then tucked it under the seat in front of them.

Once they were in the air, Jake handed the blanket to Danielle.

"Uh, thank you."

"Sometimes it gets a little cold." He opened the blanket and arranged it over her lap.

A moment later, Trey's hand strayed under the blanket and stroked along her thigh. Jake's hand stroked over her other thigh.

She glanced around nervously. The flight wasn't very full and the two seats across the aisle from them were empty, so no one could really see them.

Jake smiled at her, and she smiled back, until Trey's hand found her mound and he stroked over it—then she dropped her head back on the seat, her eyes widening a little.

"You are looking a little cold." Jake's hand slid from under the blanket and he shifted it up around her shoulders, tucking it in behind her.

Trey's fingers slipped under her panties and stroked her slit. She could feel the wetness gathering there.

"Would you like something?"

Danielle started at the sound of the stewardess's voice.

"I'll have an orange juice," Jake said as he lowered the little table to his lap. "How about you, Danielle? A soft drink or juice?"

Trey's fingers dipped inside her. "Or maybe something hot?" Trey suggested.

Hot? Yes, please!

"I'll take a tea, please," she managed to say in a steady voice. "One milk and one sugar."

The uniformed woman prepared her tea and set it on Jake's table. Fortunately, Jake must have seen her coming, and he hadn't put his hand under the blanket again after adjusting it around her shoulders. It might look a little odd that Trey's arm disappeared under the blanket, but if the stewardess noticed, she didn't show it. And, actually, she barely glanced past Jake's debonair smile.

She placed Trey's water on Jake's tray, too, then pushed her cart farther down the aisle.

Trey stroked over Danielle's slit again, and Jake's hand slipped underneath the blanket and glided under her T-shirt to stroke over her breast. Over the next little while, her companions teased and tormented her. Jake toyed with her nipples, squeezing and stroking, occasionally licking his finger to add a little moisture. Trey dabbed at her clit, then flicked it gently until she approached orgasm, then backed off until she almost pleaded for release. Each seemed to have staked out his individual territory, with Jake up top and Trey below, but occasionally, Jake's hand would glide downward and join Trey with a finger inside her, or add a tweak to her clit for good measure.

By the time they were ready to land, she damn well wanted someone to fuck her.

"Oh God, just do it," she murmured to Trey. "Make me . . ." She trailed off, afraid someone would overhear her.

"I don't think that's a good idea here." Trey sent her a devilish grin.

She, on the other hand, thought it was a damn fine idea!

Trey continued to tease her clit, but too lightly to do the trick.

"So you're just going to leave me like this?"

"Well, that depends. Didn't you say you have a car at the airport?"

Six

Danielle had never gotten off a plane so fast in her life. Rather then holding back until the end, like she usually did, she leapt up as soon as they landed and urged Jake into the aisle, just like they always told people not to do. As soon as the pilot gave the all clear to disembark, they were on their way out, then off to the luggage carousels. Danielle could barely stand still, she wanted to get to her car so badly.

"You don't have a car here?" she asked.

"No, we took a shuttle."

"I'll drive you home." She wouldn't let them get away until she was fully satisfied, and there was no way they were making out in the parking garage. Carleton Falls added only about thirty minutes to her trip home . . . and it would be well worth it.

Finally they had their luggage, and she led them to the

shuttle, which took them to the long-term parking lot. She unlocked her car, and Trey stowed the luggage in the trunk.

"I can drive if you like," Jake offered with a wink.

She thrust him the keys, then climbed into the backseat with Trey. Two seconds later, she tugged his cock from his pants and leaned down to lick it, then wrapped her lips around it. She cupped his balls and gently massaged them as she sucked on him in earnest. Then deciding to torment him as much as he'd tormented her, she pulled away and gave him a wicked grin.

She settled back in the seat. They were driving along the highway now. There was very little traffic, which was typical this time of day. Trey's hand slipped under her skirt and he found her mound. His finger slipped over her clit and he flicked it mercilessly. Oh, she was so close.

"You are so beautiful." Trey nuzzled her neck as his finger wiggled and teased.

Just as she felt waves of pleasure begin to encompass her and she gasped, he pulled away and returned her wicked smile.

"Maybe later, if you're good." Trey leaned in and gave her a gentle kiss.

Jake pulled off the highway to a side road, then pulled over.

"Time to switch drivers, Trey," he said as he opened the door.

Trey kissed her again, then shifted to the front seat. Jake got in beside her. As Trey started up the car and began driving, Jake kissed her deeply. She stroked his hard bulge, then pulled it out. The car pulled back onto the highway.

Jake tormented her in a similar fashion as the scenery rushed by. If it wasn't for the occasional car sharing the highway with them, Danielle would have ripped off his clothes and demanded he satisfy her.

Finally, the exit for Carleton Falls loomed just ahead.

Trey took the exit and followed along the river for a bit, then into town. A few moments later, they pulled into the driveway of a lovely old stone house.

"This is my house," Trey said with a wink. "I thought you might both come in for a bit."

As soon as they closed the door behind them, Danielle kicked off her shoes and dropped her purse to the floor, then slid her arms around Jake and kissed him. Passionate and needy. She tugged the tie from his hair and tangled her fingers in the long, smooth strands. His tongue slipped between her lips and he ravaged her mouth. She glided her hand over the impressive bulge in his pants.

Jake guided her to the living room and sat down on the cozy, plush couch. She knelt in front of him and pulled down his zipper, then freed his cock. She stood up and tugged her T-shirt over her shoulders and tossed it aside.

Next, she stripped off her skirt. Trey unfastened her bra as she shimmied out of her panties.

She knelt in front of Jake again and licked his cock, from base to tip.

"Mmm. Lovely," she said, enjoying the sight of his straining purple-veined cock.

Trey sat beside her and watched her tongue lave up Jake's cock again and again. She wondered if he wanted to join her. In fact, the more she thought about it, the more she wanted him to. Throughout their entire sexual free-for-all, the two men had barely touched each other—despite their long history together. She almost suggested it, but decided she didn't want to take the chance of ruining things by making it awkward. She wrapped her lips around Jake's cock and swallowed it whole.

Trey's hands stroked over her bare behind. As she dove down on Jake again, Trey knelt behind Danielle and urged her hips upward until she was on her hands and knees. He then leaned forward and . . .

"Oh . . ." She almost dropped Jake's cock at the feel of Trey's mouth on her. She licked Jake, then sucked him into her mouth again.

Trey's tongue slid into her slit and he licked. She moaned around Jake's member. Trey found her clit and she sucked Jake hard, then released him from her mouth, stroking his cock in her hand.

"Oh God, I need a cock inside me, Trey."

"If you insist."

He stood up and shed his pants, then positioned himself behind her. His thick cockhead pressed against her, then slid into her hot, slick depths. The feel of his rigid cock pushing into her made her gasp again.

She leaned forward and took Jake deep into her mouth and sucked him in earnest as Trey pulled out, then thrust forward again. In and out. He pounded into her. She sucked Jake, trying to concentrate as Trey fucked her like crazy, hammering into her faster and faster.

She clutched the base of Jake's cock in her hand and sucked for all she was worth as pleasure bombarded her senses. She squeezed Trey's cock within her, feeling the orgasm build. Jake groaned and filled her mouth with hot liquid. Just in time. She let him slip from her mouth as she wailed her own release, bliss exploding within her like a supernova. Trey groaned and thrust some more, and then he, too, erupted inside her.

Oh God, these men were incredible.

She wanted Jake again. Now.

When she shifted, Trey slid from behind her. Danielle sat down on the floor, then stretched out on the carpet and stared up at Jake, opening her arms.

"Jake?"

He stared at his flaccid member. "I'm going to need a minute."

He wrapped his hand around his cock and she stroked her breasts and tweaked her nipples to help him along.

"I think I can give a hand." Trey sat down beside Jake and wrapped his hand around Jake's cock. The sight made Danielle even hotter . . . and it seemed to have a powerful effect on Jake, because as Trey stroked him, Jake's cock swelled to full attention in record time.

Trey released him and Jake dropped to his knees, then prowled over Danielle. His curtain of hair streamed across her shoulder as he took her lips in a fast, hard kiss, then drove his cock into her in one forward thrust.

She moaned, loving his long, hard cock inside her. She wrapped her arms and legs around him and met his every thrust as he ground into her again and again.

"Oh, yeah, baby. Fuck me hard," she cried.

His cock speared into her again and again and she arched against him as she felt the waves of pleasure swell.

"I'm so close. Jake, you're going to make me . . ."

He thrust, kissing her neck. Then he swirled around and thrust deep.

She plummeted over the edge . . . into the free-fall of bliss. He held her, and kept pumping, as she moaned and moaned through an orgasm that seemed to last forever.

He groaned and thrust several more times, and then they simply clung to each other as they caught their breath. She sighed, hearing her pulse thumping past her ears.

Good heavens, these men had spoiled her for having sex with only one man again.

Or any man other than them.

Danielle woke up to a warm male chest pressed against her cheek and curly hair tickling her nose. She stroked her cheek against his chest and sighed.

"Morning, sleepyhead." Jake kissed the top of her head.

"Mmm." She realized there was no warm male body behind her. She glanced over her shoulder. "Where's Trey?"

"He had to go to work."

"Poor Trey. What about you?"

"I have a more flexible schedule than he does. Want some breakfast?"

"You offering to make it?" She loved breakfast, but she hated preparing it. Left to her own, she'd just have cereal.

"Sure. How about eggs Benedict?"

"Sounds good to me." She slipped out of bed and headed to the shower.

After she finished drying her hair and dressing, she walked into the kitchen. Jake handed her a red stoneware mug filled with steaming coffee. She glanced around the bright kitchen with its light-stained wooden cabinets and tiled countertops. There was a cozy little breakfast nook surrounded by windows overlooking a treed backyard where birds chirped cheerfully.

She sat down and gazed outside to enjoy the view. Trey's bike sat on one side of the large wooden deck.

"I'm surprised Trey didn't ride his bike to work."

"He did." Jake glanced up and saw the direction of her gaze. "Ah, he has more than one bike."

She sipped her coffee as she watched Jake move around Trey's kitchen with ease. He flipped the bacon, then continued to whisk the sauce in a metal bowl.

"Do you want me to set the table?" she asked.

"No, you just sit there looking gorgeous. I'll handle it."

She sipped more hot coffee. That's what she liked. A man who could handle himself in the kitchen *and* in the bedroom!

Less than fifteen minutes later, he set a great-looking plate of eggs Benedict in front of her, then sat across from her.

"This looks great." She took a bite and crooned. "And it tastes even better."

"I aim to please."

And he did. In every way.

She ate a few more bites, then decided to broach the subject she'd been so curious about. "So what happened with you and Trey? You seemed so happy when you were together."

Jake glanced at her, then shrugged. "It was a college romance." He took a sip of his orange juice.

"That doesn't mean it can't last."

Jake nodded as he took a bite of his food. "That's true but . . . You know, I always knew that I was attracted to both men and women. Trey . . . he knew he was attracted to men, and he assumed that meant he was . . . only attracted to men. When we met at college, he and I hit it off, we were both attracted to each other . . . and we wound up together. And it was great . . . but we came to realize that something was missing in our relationship. When our friends Nikki and Angela agreed to share a town house with us, Trey started to realize that he was attracted to women, too."

Last night, before the three of them had made love for the first time, Trey had mentioned that both he and Jake had been curious about making love to her when they'd been together. It must have been just a mild interest; otherwise wouldn't they have acted on it?

"What happened with your roommates? Did Trey end up with one of them?"

"Well . . . sort of. He walked in on Nikki coming out of the shower one day. She noticed he was turned on and she did what came naturally."

Her eyes widened. "So you caught them in the bathroom making out? You must have been devastated."

He smiled. "No, more like turned on. I joined them. Angela got in on the action soon afterward, and we had a great foursome going on."

She stared at him in amazement. Had it really been that easy for him to move forward? The discussion with Trey that he felt an attraction to her would have given Jake some warning, but still . . .

"Sorry to shock you, Danielle. After the past two nights, I assumed you'd be okay with this, but I need to remember this isn't your usual thing."

"No, it's not that. I'm just surprised that you and Trey never got back together. After you started this thing with Nikki and Angela, did the sex between you and Trey stop?"

"As an exclusive thing, yes. We really focused on the women, just like we do with you."

She could tell by the sadness in his eyes that he was putting on a brave face. She was sure of it. And he would have done the same for Trey, too. Jake had always tended to put other people's needs ahead of his own.

She pursed her lips. "You know, it doesn't have to be that way."

"I know . . . but Trey . . . he was searching for his sexual identity. I took my cue from him, knowing he needed to find his way. He did."

"So he pursues strictly females now?"

"You'd have to ask him that. We live in the same town, but we don't see each other all that often. We get together for the occasional meal, but mostly, we just spend time together on our yearly vacations with some of the others from Carleton Falls U."

Danielle chewed her lower lip. "You still care about him, though, don't you?"

"Of course I care about him. He's my friend."

"I mean more than that." She rested her hand on his. "Are you still in love with him?"

He drew his hand away and took a sip of his coffee. A moment later, he gazed at her sheepishly. "Is it that obvious?"

"Why don't you try getting together again?"

"Look, Danielle, I know you're trying to help, but . . ."

"Okay. Sorry, I don't mean to be pushy. I know it's hard to pick up a relationship again. But it's such a shame that you hardly even see each other anymore. You two always seemed so perfect for each other."

"That's because we were. But a lot of time has gone by, and when it comes down to it, if Trey really wanted to be with me, he would have found his way back."

"How about if I come up a few times on weekends this summer and the three of us spend time together?" she suggested. "Then at least you could revitalize your friendship."

Smiling, he took her hand. "You know, Danielle, you don't need an excuse to come and visit. I love being with you."

Her cheeks flushed. "Oh, well . . . uh, how about I come up next Friday and stay the weekend? I'll make dinner for you on Friday and you can invite Trey over to join us. Then we'll go from there."

He nodded. "That sounds like a great idea."

Jake turned the key in the lock and pushed open the front door. That wonderful thank-God-it's-Friday-and-the-weekend's-begun feeling wafted through him, but with a bright twinkle of anticipation knowing Danielle would be arriving soon.

Her conversation last week about him and Trey had dredged up the familiar pain. For years, he'd hoped that Trey would figure things out and come to terms with the fact that he could love a man. Jake had always known he loved Trey, and he had prayed that Trey would realize he loved Jake, too, and want him back. But Jake had finally given up hope when it became clear that ever since Trey found he enjoyed sex with women, too, he seemed determined to find a woman to love.

This past week, though, painful thoughts of what Jake had lost with Trey, which always haunted him after spending any significant time with him, had been replaced by vibrant memories of making love with Danielle.

He couldn't believe how much he'd missed her this past week. Every redheaded co-ed that had sat in his classroom or come to his office to ask about this week's assignment had reminded him of Danielle. Not that any of those young girls had tempted him. They just sent memories swirling through his mind of how beautiful Danielle had been in college with her delicate, shy demeanor, and that made him think how even more beautiful she was now that she was a woman who'd shed those reserved ways and fully embraced her womanhood.

His groin ached at the memory of her lovely face glowing in orgasm as he and Trey had brought her there together last Sunday. He put his briefcase down on the floor as he unfastened his shoes and placed them on the mat by the closet. He opened the sliding door and placed his briefcase inside.

"Good evening, Master Jamieson."

Seven

Jake started at the sound of Danielle's voice, then sucked in a breath when he saw her standing ten feet away in the most sexy maid's outfit he'd ever seen. Short. Baring white thighs for about an inch above the long black stockings held up by black lace garters. His gaze glided down her legs to the impossibly high spiked heels she wore.

He whistled.

"Would you like me to pour you a beer, Master Jamieson?"

Ah, so she was going to play out the role of his maid, and probably a very willing one at that.

"Yes, thank you . . . Dani."

She smiled and curtsied. God she was adorable. The widely flared black skirt with the white lacy petticoat bounced with life. And the front of the bodice was laced to just under her breasts, the garment tight around her body.

There the black garment ended and the white undergarment flared over her full breasts, which were pushed up where the deep scoop of the neckline revealed a delightful swell of white flesh and her creamy bare shoulders. She'd fastened her long auburn hair into a fancy coil at the back of her head, but curly tendrils framed her face.

She turned around and his heart rate quickened at the way the black skirt tapered upward at the back, revealing rows and rows of lace on the white undergarment barely covering her derriere. His gaze remained glued to that enticing, swaying lace as she walked toward the kitchen. He stopped at the kitchen door as he watched her retrieve one of his glass beer mugs from the freezer drawer at the bottom of his stainless-steel fridge and set it on the counter. She must have put that mug in there, because he kept them up in the cupboard. The glass frosted in the warmer air of the room as she opened a tall green bottle of imported beer and poured it into the cold mug. She set it on the end of the long black marble counter, so he sat down on the stool in front of it and took a sip.

She smiled and curtsied again, then turned around and crossed to the stainless-steel stove, where he saw she had a large glass casserole dish with a lid sitting on the glossy black cooking surface. She opened the oven and leaned forward to put the casserole inside. As her skirt tipped upward, revealing more of her upper thighs, she shifted her weight from one foot to the other, sending the lacy skirt bouncing slightly. As she leaned further still, her skirt bounced upward to reveal . . . lovely, creamy round mounds framing a narrow black triangle of silk between. He almost groaned. She was wearing a black thong . . . under that short, enticing skirt. Now as she moved around, he'd be constantly anticipating a glimpse of her sexy derriere. It would be sheer torment. And he was looking forward to every second of it.

She stood up and closed the oven door, then turned around and faced him. "Is there anything else I can do for you, Master Jamieson?"

"Uh . . . yes, Dani, would you check that bottom drawer for my . . . uh, car keys."

It was all he could think of in his current befuddled state, but she smiled and curtsied.

"Of course, Master Jamieson."

She turned around and leaned over, revealing even more delightful derriere as she bent at the waist, then shifted back and forth a little, sending her skirt bouncing as she scoured that drawer, sifting through the towels for the nonexistent car keys. His cock swelled at the sight of her naked behind framed by that bouncing white lace and black overskirt.

Finally, she stood up and turned to face him. Satisfaction gleamed in her emerald eyes at his intense gaze. "Sorry, sir, they don't seem to be there."

"Ah, then maybe you could check the top cupboard." He pointed at the glass-doored cupboard over the sink.

She opened the door and stretched upward. The movement caused her skirt to shift upward, revealing more creamy thigh. Finally, she grabbed a box from the top shelf and pulled it down. She turned and walked toward him, a sexy sway to her hips.

"Sorry, sir. No keys." She handed him the box and he saw they were cookies.

"Why did you give me these?" he asked.

"Because I thought you might like something sweet." As she stared at him, she licked her lips. She stood a mere foot from him. Too far away.

He thumped the cookies down on the counter, his hormones thrumming through him.

He stood up. She shifted a little, but their bodies nearly touched.

"I would like something sweet, but not cookies."

She stared up at him, anticipation glimmering in her eyes, obviously waiting for a kiss, but instead, he pushed the box of cookies back into her hand.

"Put these away . . . there." He pointed to the bottom cupboard and followed her across the kitchen. When she leaned over to place the box away, his hand stroked up the back of her thigh, then under her skirt and over her round, firm flesh.

"You have a lovely ass, Dani."

"Thank you, sir."

He stroked her several more times, then wrapped

his hands around her waist and stroked upward until just under her breasts, then drew her up from her bent position. His hands cupped her full breasts. They filled his palms, the nipples jutting forward into his hold. He drew her back against his chest as he gently squeezed and stroked those lovely breasts. She rested her head against his shoulder and the delightful scent of her mango shampoo filled his nostrils. He breathed in, savoring the sweetness, then nuzzled her temple. Her soft auburn curls caressed his cheek.

"You're incredibly beautiful, Dani."

"Thank you, Master Jamieson."

He turned her around and smiled as she gazed up at him with glittering green eyes. He lowered his face to hers and kissed her. The delicate feel of her lips on his was sweet and sensuous, then turned more passionate as her tongue stroked along his lips, then dove inside with enthusiasm. He stroked her tongue, then drew it deeper into his mouth. Her lips moved on his with an eager breathlessness.

She drew away and gazed up at him, blatant need in her eyes. Her hand stroked over his throbbing bulge.

"Sir, you look a little uncomfortable. Allow me."

She tugged on his belt buckle and released the tab. A second later, she had his zipper undone and her delicate fingers wrapped around his cock.

"Ohhhh . . . that's much better," he said.

She stroked him up and down. He ached to drive his cock inside her wet opening, but he resisted the blind animal drive so he could enjoy the playful, and intensely sexy, foreplay. She leaned forward and at the first touch of her hot, damp tongue on his cockhead, he groaned. She licked him from base to tip and he stroked her head affectionately. Soon she wrapped her lips around him and took his cockhead into her warm mouth.

"Oh, sweetheart, that feels wonderful."

She sucked and licked, driving him wild. Within moments, she had him ready to burst at the seams, so he stilled her head.

"Okay, honey, it's time to stop. As much as I love your delightful mouth, there's somewhere else I'd like to be right now."

Dani released him and stood up, her sultry gaze telling him she'd like a few things right now, too. She wrapped her arms around his neck and kissed him, then sucked and licked his lips, driving him wild. He pressed back on her shoulders and decided to take control again. After all, that's the scenario she'd set up.

He gazed at her lovely face, then reached around and opened the barrette holding her hair in the coil at the back of her head. Her hair tumbled around her shoulders. He ran his fingers through the silky strands, then smoothed it around her shoulders.

"Dani, go and check what's in the oven."

"Yes, sir." She turned and crossed to the oven, then flicked on the oven light and leaned over.

He followed her and stroked her upper thighs, then glided under her skirt and caressed her round cheeks. Then he wrapped his hands around her waist and shifted her sideways, away from the stove to an area of open counter. She grasped the edge as he returned to stroking her round ass, then glided one hand between her thighs. As soon as he glided his fingers over the silky fabric of her thong, he felt her wetness. It had soaked right through the delicate fabric.

He grinned, gliding his hands up her body, cupping her breasts. He toyed with her nipples, then dipped one hand under her neckline and inside her bra cup to find her hard nipple. She moaned. He tugged the fabric down, both her bodice and the lace of her bra cups, baring both breasts, then tugged and squeezed her nipples until she moaned again.

He couldn't take it any longer. He slid his hands under her skirt and found the elastic waistband of her thong and drew it down her long legs, dropping it to the floor. She kicked it aside as he eased her thighs wider. He stroked his member along her lovely ass, then nudged between her legs. She leaned forward, stretching her torso over the countertop.

"Oh," she yelped softly.

"Something wrong?" he asked in concern.

"No, sir, it's just the marble is cold."

He touched her nipples. They were exceptionally hard and distended.

"Would you like a towel to rest on?" he asked.

"No, it's . . . sexy."

He laughed, but the thought of her soft breasts pressed flat on the hard, cold marble sent his cock throbbing even more. He stroked along her wet slit, then placed his cockhead against her again and eased forward. Her slick vagina swallowed him, inch by heavenly inch. When he was finally fully immersed in her heat, he held her tight against him, afraid to move because he was so . . . so close.

"Oh, Master Jamieson, please fuck me."

That was it. He drew back, then rammed into her. His balls tightened and he thrust again, then again. Heat blasted through him as he erupted into her hot, tight pussy. She moaned and gasped.

Before he could soften, he pulled free, spun her around, and lifted her onto the countertop. She gasped again, probably at the cold, hard marble under her, but he quickly drove into her again. He stroked her clit as he thrust. She clung to his shoulders.

"Oh God, sir. You're going to make me . . . ahh . . ." She moaned. "I'm coming again." Her voice trailed to a moan, then she wailed as she held on to him.

He watched her face as she came. Her mass of auburn curls framed her flushed face like a halo, her emerald eyes glazed in passion, and her full lips parted as she uttered sweet sounds of pleasure.

She relaxed in his arms, and smiled up at him. "Thank you, Master Jamieson."

"My pleasure, Dani." He held her close and kissed her, not wanting to part from her warm feminine body yet.

She stroked his hair, then rested her head against his shoulder for several long, tender moments.

Finally, she drew away and smiled at him again. "Master Jamieson, will your friend Master Garner be here soon?"

That had been the plan. For Trey to join them for dinner.

"I told him I'd call."

She stroked her hand over her bare breast. "How soon do you think he can arrive?"

"Oh, I think he could get here pretty fast."

He slipped free of her lovely hot body, then grabbed the phone hanging from the wall. As he watched her rearrange her maid outfit, tucking her lovely breasts away under the white fabric, he wondered if he actually wanted to share her.

Even with Trey.

Trey hesitated outside Jake's front door. Jake had called him saying to come over right away because he had a surprise for him. Trey had only been to Jake's house a few times. The distance between him and Jake saddened Trey, but he understood that Jake needed that distance. Their romantic relationship hadn't had a distinct end, since they'd contin-ued to meet up—and play—with Angela and Nikki once a year. Trey always had the feeling Jake hoped they would eventually get back together again. Even after all these years . . . Maybe maintaining such a casual physical rela-tionship wasn't such a great idea . . . but Trey sure didn't want to give that up. And he was sure Jake didn't either.

Jake had told him Danielle intended to come over this weekend and had invited him over for dinner this eve-ning . . . later this evening . . . but it seemed Danielle had arrived earlier than Jake had expected. The odd thing was Jake had asked Trey to call a few minutes before he ar-rived, and then just to let himself in.

They were probably having sex and wanted a warning before Trey got there—which for some reason made Trey a little jealous—but why tell him to let himself in?

He wrapped his hand around the doorknob. Should he knock before he entered? Damn, he was just overthinking things. He pushed the door open and stepped inside.

Eight

"I'm here . . ."

Trey's voice trailed off as he saw Danielle, dressed in a skimpy, and very sexy, maid's outfit, with her hands above her head. He quickly closed the door behind him and locked it.

"I . . . uh . . ."

Suddenly, he realized that her hands were above her head because they were tied together with a rope which was then twined through the rising banister behind her, holding them high above her head. As his gaze glided down her sexily clad form, taking in her voluptuous breasts spilling from the low neckline, her slim waistline, then her legs skewed wide, his cock hardened.

Oh man, she was sitting and . . . two male legs jutted out from between her thighs, and he realized she was sitting on Jake's lap, her feet curled around the dark cherrywood legs of one of Jake's stylishly elegant dining room chairs beneath them.

"Trey, I'm glad you're here." Jake peered out from behind Danielle's head. "My maid, Dani, here has been very bad, and I wanted you to help me punish her."

"Punish her?" Trey stepped closer, his groin tightening painfully. "Okay."

He wanted to say more . . . to ask about her misdeed . . . but he couldn't stop staring at her skirt . . . wondering what was happening under there. Was Jake's long cock pressing close against her? Was it . . . inside her?

"Say hello to Master Garner, Dani."

"Hello, Master Garner."

Master. Oh God, that was sexy.

As he stood in front of her, he wanted to reach out and grab those lovely round breasts, which thrust forward so beautifully between her upraised arms. Jake caressed one lovely mound, then tugged the fabric down to reveal a hardened nipple. Trey stroked a finger over the nub and Danielle moaned softly. He leaned forward and licked it, then squeezed his lips around it, teasing the tip with his tongue. The aureole pebbled against his lips. Her accelerated breathing sent his pulse racing.

Jake pulled up her full but very short skirt, revealing her naked pussy. Trey's eyes widened. At this angle, it looked like . . . Trey stepped back and confirmed that Jake's hard cock was inside her.

He could imagine Jake's hard cock, veins bulging, pressed deep inside her . . . Danielle squeezing him tight.

Oh God, his cock throbbed in his pants.

"You're looking uncomfortable there, buddy. Why not loosen things up a bit?" Jake said.

Trey unfastened his pants, knowing that's what Jake was alluding to. He dropped them to the floor, then released his rock-hard cock from his briefs. Danielle's gaze rested on his erection, her shimmering green eyes filled with hunger.

He stepped closer, wanting her full, sexy lips to wrap around his cockhead, but sitting on Jake's lap like that . . . *his cock inside her* . . . she was too high to reach him, and her arms tied to the banister didn't allow her to bend down.

For a moment, he considered offering his cock to Jake. The thought of Jake pleasuring both Danielle and him at the same time was an intense turn-on.

"Use the step stool," Jake suggested. "It's right there." His head gestured to the right.

Trey glanced around and saw the dark cherrywood step stool Jake usually kept under the desk in the kitchen sitting two feet to the right of Jake and Danielle. Obviously, Jake had thought this through.

Trey placed the stool in position and stepped on top of it. Danielle stroked her cheek against his cock, licking the side of it. Her soft skin, then warm tongue made his cock twitch in delight. Jake grasped Trey's cock in his firm, masculine grip and stroked a couple of times . . . fracturing

Trey's composure. . . . Then Jake positioned Trey's cock in front of Danielle's mouth.

It had been a long time since Trey had felt Jake's touch there and it sent strong bittersweet memories surging forward. A gnawing ache began deep inside him . . . until Danielle's mouth surrounded his tip while her tongue toyed with the small opening on the end of him. Slowly, Jake fed Trey's cock into her mouth. She swirled her tongue around his shaft as it eased deeper inside. Once it was as far as it would go, her cheeks hollowed as she sucked on him. Jake drew him out, then eased him in again. A slow rhythm . . . in . . . out . . . felt superbly erotic.

Then Jake drew him all the way out and Jake's lips surrounded him. His teeth edged lightly around Trey's corona, then Jake swallowed him deep. With Trey's cock deep inside Jake's mouth, Jake lifted Trey's balls and pressed them to Danielle's mouth. She licked them, then Jake fed one into her mouth. She cradled it inside her warmth and Trey moaned. Jake fed the other ball into her mouth and she laved her tongue over them. As Danielle sucked on his balls, Jake moved up and down Trey's shaft. Trey wanted to move, to fuck Jake's mouth like old times, but if he did, he'd pull free of Danielle's mouth, and he didn't want that.

Jake sped up and Trey felt the familiar tightening in his groin—then he burst in an intense, carnal climax, groaning loudly.

God, he and Jake hadn't shared such personal intimacy

in a long time and . . . he was surprised how much Jake still turned him on. Had he only been fooling himself that he was over Jake? Or was it just that Danielle heightened everything about the sexual experience? All he knew right now was that being with both of them was more intensely erotic than anything he'd ever experienced before.

Jake released him, smiling broadly.

"You know, I think Dani still needs her lesson. Right, Dani?"

"Yes, Master Jamieson."

Trey stepped down and pushed the step stool away. Jake's hand toyed with his cock, which still impaled Danielle.

"Let me make some room for you," Jake said. He lifted Danielle, drew out his cock, then repositioned it. Slowly, he lowered Danielle again, his cock pushing inside her ass.

Trey's own cock rose at the sight. He reached around Danielle and felt for her bra fastening through the fabric, then unhooked it and pulled it from inside her dress. He tossed the strapless scrap of lace aside, then pulled the fabric of her top down and tucked it under her breasts. He admired the lovely round mounds, then leaned down and captured Danielle's nipple inside his mouth and sucked until she moaned loudly.

"You should feel how wet she is," Jake said. His hand stroked her glistening pussy.

Trey knelt in front of her and stroked her slit. Oh man,

it was totally hot and wet. He slipped a couple of fingers into the silky wetness inside.

"Do you want me inside you, Danielle?" he asked.

"Oh, yes, Master Garner. Please fuck me."

Urgency spiked through him at those words. He placed the step stool in front of her, then grabbed his cock, placed it to her opening, and thrust forward. Her velvety pussy surrounded him and he groaned. The sensation was intensified knowing Jake's cock had just been in the same place.

"Fuck her, Trey. Let's make her come together."

Oh, yeah. He pulled back, then thrust again, deeper this time.

"Ohhh . . . Please, masters, make me come."

He thrust faster. Deeper. She squeezed him and he groaned, then sped up. Her breath came in little gasps and he pounded in . . . harder and harder.

"Oh, yes. I'm going to . . ." She sucked in a breath, then wailed long and hard.

His groin tightened as Jake groaned his release. Heat burned through him as he exploded within her, thrusting and groaning as she wailed again.

"I'm . . . coming . . . oh . . ." She gasped. "So . . . hard."

Trey tweaked her clit and she wailed again.

As her cries subsided, he slowed his thrusts. Finally, her head dropped against his shoulder. He cupped her head and held it lovingly, kissing her temple and savoring the blissful moment they all shared.

"So you couldn't stay away from us." Trey curled his hands around Danielle's slender waist as she placed the steaming casserole on the hot plate she'd set on the counter beside Jake's shiny-topped stainless-steel stove, then closed the oven door. She wore one of Jake's T-shirts, which hung just long enough to cover the tiny pink thong she wore underneath. She turned around and kissed him, her arms gliding around his neck, the black quilted oven mitts still covering her hands.

"How could I? You two have a way of making a girl feel special." She kissed him again. Her lovely green eyes gazed up at him as a grin spread across her face. "Very special."

"Well, you are." He kissed her again, hardly able to keep his hands from roving over her delightful body and taking her again right there on the spot. He'd never had it this bad for a woman before. "After all, how many women would dress up in a sexy little maid's outfit and serve the two of us . . . and so completely?"

He couldn't help it . . . his hand cupped her breast. The soft flesh filled his palm and the nipple tightened and pressed against him.

"Hey, you're hogging the woman," Jake said as he cupped her other breast.

Trey released her, and Jake pulled her into his arms and kissed her. She smiled up at him with the same delighted expression she'd given Trey a second before, and Trey couldn't help feeling a little jealousy. An emotion he immediately stomped down.

Trey tugged the oven mitts from her hands, ignoring how her fingers immediately stroked through Jake's long hair, hanging loose past his shoulders. Trey donned the mitts, then carried the casserole into the dining room. Jake appeared with a bottle of wine and a corkscrew, then set about removing the cork while Danielle placed fine crystal wineglasses on the table by each white porcelain plate with a burgundy band around the edge trimmed in gold. Gold flatware completed the place settings.

"I hope you like it. It's a curried chicken and rice casserole . . . my own recipe," she said.

"It smells delicious." Trey sat down at the round table with Danielle to his right and Jake to his left, soft light from tall tapered candles in crystal star-shaped holders setting the table aglow.

"So, Danielle, do you make dinner for men often?" Trey asked.

She picked up a big serving spoon and placed it into the casserole, then scooped some onto her plate. "Not really." She smiled. "I've never been involved with two men at the same time before."

Trey smiled, knowing she was avoiding his question. He wanted to know if she'd gone out with a lot of men . . .

and if she'd ever fallen in love. She'd had a rough time growing up—being all alone—and although he wanted her to be happy, the thought of her in love with someone else bothered him. Probably because he couldn't stand the thought of her heart being broken.

But even more . . . he wanted to know if she thought he . . . and Jake . . . were special.

"What do you do for fun?" Jake asked.

"Oh, um . . . Well, I like reading manga."

"You mean Japanese comics?" Jake took a bite of his dinner.

"Well, sure, but some of the story lines are very complex and they cover a broad range of story types."

Trey grinned at her defensiveness. "I know that women dressed in various costumes and uniforms are popular in manga. Is that where you got the idea for the maid outfit?"

Her cheeks stained pink as she nodded.

"What else do you like to do?" Jake asked.

"Well, I play online games. You know . . . where you become a character in a simulated world and interact with other people doing the same thing. It's really quite fascinating. You can live a whole alternate life there. Be whatever you want. Do whatever you want."

Trey watched her as she focused on her food while she talked. And by interacting with people online, she could totally avoid interacting with real people. He had a strong feeling she spent most of her spare time hiding from the world, and he doubted she dated much. Yet, she didn't seem shy about sex.

"Have you had any serious relationships?" Trey asked.

She took a bite of her food, then chewed slowly. "No, not really. I mean, I did date a guy for about eight months once, but his company transferred him to New York and it sort of ended. Mostly I keep it pretty casual." She shrugged and took a sip of her wine. "I mean, I've got my life pretty well set. I don't really need a man. Except for sex, of course."

"Of course." Jake raised an eyebrow at Trey.

Jake seemed to understand as clearly as Trey did that Danielle would not readily let someone into her life, because she would be afraid of depending on that relationship, then possibly losing it and being left all alone again.

"If it's sex you're looking for, does that mean these visits could become a regular thing?" Trey asked.

She picked up her burgundy linen napkin and smoothed it across her lap. "Well, would you like them to be?"

How could she sound so doubtful, as if she thought he might tell her no?

Trey glanced at Jake, then back to Danielle. "Absolutely. I think it would be great. How about next weekend you stay at my place?"

The light breeze brushed across Danielle's cheeks, her hair swirling behind her as she pedaled the borrowed bicycle along the river. The tiny ripples on the surface of the water glittered in the afternoon sun, and the tall trees, the leaves rustling softly, sent dappled sunlight along the smooth gray surface of the bike path.

She had forgotten how beautiful it was here. The combination of the lovely setting and the pleasant heart-pumping activity made her feel vibrantly alive. Her gaze strayed to Trey and Jake riding alongside her, wearing shorts and T-shirts. And the view of hard male muscle and tight buns didn't hurt either.

As they reached the top of the current rise, the library tower from the university came into view between the trees along the shore, off to their left. Then, through a clearing in the trees, she could see the whole campus laid out below them. The sprawling psychology building, the blocky fortress that was the mathematics and computer science building, the chemistry and biology buildings linked by glass walkways. And new buildings she didn't recognize.

"Those are the new residences they built about five years ago," Jake said, noticing her gaze.

She nodded, remembering how difficult it had been for students to find a place to live. Building those residences would have been a godsend to the students here . . . yet the change bothered her. Things had been perfect the way they'd been. Now things had changed.

They continued to ride, the downward slope making it a fast, easy pace. The small blocky forms in the distance grew to life-sized multistoried buildings. They crossed Riverside Road, then past the southernmost parking lot, then along the main path across campus. A few students sat along the small lake—more like a large pond, actually—feeding the ducks. Attendance was light during the summer, she remembered.

"Do you want to go see Hanover House?" Trey asked.

That was where Danielle had shared a residence room with Harmony. Where she had found her first real friend . . . a friend she'd let slip through her fingers as soon as she'd left this place.

"I talked to the administrator last week and he said we could go in and see your old room."

"I . . . uh . . . don't know."

"Why don't we grab a beer at the pub first?" Jake suggested.

"That sounds like a great idea." She could use a drink before rousing any more memories from her past.

The pub hadn't changed much in all these years. They walked down the stairs to a dimly lit room of round tables each surrounded by chairs, anywhere from three to six per table. While here, one wouldn't know if it was sunny or snow-ridden outside. No outside light penetrated the Cave, as it was called.

Trey and Danielle sat down while Jake wandered toward the bar. Only one other table was occupied. A young man and woman, books spread out on the table in front of them as they sipped beer from pilsner glasses.

Jake plunked a pitcher of beer in front of them, then put down a tower of three glasses. He unstacked them, then tipped the pitcher to fill each with the amber, fuzzy liquid.

She hadn't had beer in years, but the bitter, yeasty taste reminded her of good times spent with people who had been her friends—including the two men at her side. She sipped again, the cold beer refreshing after the long ride here. She hadn't liked beer when she'd arrived at university, but it was affordable, especially with a pitcher shared with others . . . and made her feel part of the crowd. She'd liked that feeling. So she'd acquired a taste for beer.

"So, Jake, you said you teach now," said Danielle. "Math, right?"

Jake shook his head.

She raised an eyebrow. "Computers?"

Trey chuckled. "You'll never guess."

That could only mean one thing. "No, you don't teach philosophy?"

"That's the one," Jake confirmed.

"But you always liked subjects with definite right or wrong answers. Things that didn't have shades of gray." Then she remembered that logic and artificial intelligence had been areas of study included under philosophy. "Of course, you pursued your interest in AI, right?"

"Not exactly. Except as a study in ethics. Should intelligent machines be created, and if they were, would they have souls?"

"Okay. That really is a change."

As she gazed into his eyes, she realized he'd probably gone searching for answers. When he'd lost Trey, he might have been seeking an understanding of why people behave the way they do. Why people accept some things and reject others. Like Trey being afraid to embrace his sexual orientation. Like society's long history of rebuffing same-sex couples. Like even when people accepted an alternate sexual orientation, they often still required that the people in question choose one gender or the other, asserting that the very real feelings bisexuals have for those of their same gender are a choice, rather than an inherent and totally spontaneous desire they have no control over.

Being bisexual must be a confusing and difficult path . . . made more difficult for Jake because even his lover, Trey, couldn't accept what they had. Trey's discovery that he was bisexual seemed to allow him to deny his desire for Jake—or any man—and embrace what he felt was a normal, or more acceptable and safer, type of relationship. Heterosexuality.

It must have been a terrible blow to Jake, despite his apparent calm acceptance, to lose someone he'd cherished so deeply. And still did.

As they stepped into the bright afternoon, Danielle noticed that dark clouds threatened the edges of the glorious blue sky. Before they'd left Jake's house, they'd stuffed towels and bathing suits into their backpacks in hopes of enjoying a swim after their visit to campus.

"Maybe we should skip that swim and head back," she suggested. She didn't even mention going to her old residence, hoping they'd forget about that entirely.

"Nonsense," Trey said. "It's not much farther. Anyway, a little rain won't hurt us."

When she was younger, she used to love being out in the rain. She glanced at the darkening sky. Was she becoming stodgy?

"Okay, let's go." She began pedaling and the men fell in beside her.

About fifteen minutes later, they turned off the main bike path to one winding through the woods. Ten minutes after that, with still a good twenty minutes of uphill riding to their destination—a swimming hole in a small clearing—the sky began pelting them with large, heavy droplets of rain. Slowly, at first, her shirt splotched with large, wet stains. . . . Then the drops came faster, until she was drenched.

"Nice view," Trey kidded.

Her bra was totally visible through the light cotton

shirt. Of course, she didn't mind the view of Trey's shirt clinging to his awesome tight abs.

A flash of lightning lit the sky and a sharp crack of thunder nearly sent her flying off the bike. Lightning flashed again, followed by a rolling boom across the distance. Shivers ran through her, as much from the pyrotechnics as from the chill of the air traveling across her wet body.

"Maybe we should find some shelter," Jake said. "Trey, where's that cave?"

"Not too far."

They rode a little farther, then Trey pointed ahead.

"See the break in the trees there?" He rode ahead a bit, then stopped and dismounted.

Danielle and Jake slowed and stopped beside him.

"It's over this way." Jake walked his bike between the trees, then along a narrow walking path. They followed until they came to a sharp, rocky rise.

"Over here." Trey grabbed his backpack, which had been fastened to the back of his bike, and flung it over his shoulders. Jake grabbed Danielle's pack and his own, and they followed Trey.

Danielle wasn't too sure about the idea of taking shelter in a dark, dingy cave, the thought of bats and other subterranean creatures stirring disturbing fears.

When she saw the wide, fairly open, but sheltered area under the rock overhang, she sighed in relief. The area was about twelve feet wide, surrounded on three sides by rock walls and inset about eight feet under the rock overhang. She could cope with this.

She stepped inside the shelter, followed by Jake. Trey dropped his backpack on the ground and unzipped it. He tugged out a rolled blanket and spread it out on the ground, then produced a couple of beach towels, which he tossed on the blanket, still folded. They looked like comfy cushions to sit on.

She heard the zip of Jake's bag behind her.

"You're drenched," he said.

She felt soft terry cloth as Jake dropped a towel over her head, then proceeded to dry her hair.

When he freed her head from his towel-handed grip, she noticed that Trey had removed his sopping wet shirt.

Jake dropped the towel, then pulled his shirt off, too.

"You know, you really should take that wet shirt off." Jake's blue eyes glinted, enhancing his totally devilish grin.

"I could do that, but then you'd see me in only my bra." She smiled. "We couldn't have that." She reached under the back of her shirt and unfastened her bra, tugged the loop of one strap past her elbow and worked her arm free, then did the same with the other side. . . . Then she reached under the front of her shirt and tugged the bra down and out.

Both men's gazes glued to her breasts, which she was aware might as well have been naked given the wet, nearly transparent fabric clinging to them. It was totally sexy knowing she was totally covered by the shirt . . . yet hid nothing.

"You're right. That's much better," Trey said.

She wriggled out of her shorts and tossed them to the side, then turned and knelt down while she positioned a towel, quite aware she was flashing them an eyeful of practically naked derriere. She shifted around, then stretched out on the blanket, her head resting on the towel.

"Mmm. Maybe it's a good time for a nap. I'm a little cold, though."

Both men pounced to her side, then wrapped their arms around her, cocooning her between them.

"Do you think the rain will last long?" she asked.

"I certainly hope so," Trey said as his hand strayed under her shirt and up her stomach, then covered her cold breast.

"And in the meantime, I wouldn't mind something to nibble on." Jake sat up and leaned toward her. His mouth covered her hard, aching nipple through the cloth, and she sighed as the heat surrounded her.

She stroked her hand over the front of Jake's shorts, finding a growing bulge. Her hand found Trey, and he guided her hand inside his already open fly to wrap around his hardening cock, still surrounded by the light cotton of his boxers. He held her hand in place as he disposed of his shorts, then shifted her hand briefly as he pulled away the boxers. She grasped his hot hard cock again and squeezed.

Jake drew away, then stood up to dispose of his remaining clothes. Danielle noticed a few large rocks along the side of the cave, big enough to sit on.

"Over there." She pointed. "Sit on that rock."

Both men, naked, rippling muscles glistening with moisture, sat beside each other on the largest rock. She knelt in front of them and grasped each of their cocks in her hand. She pressed them together and licked the tips, so hard and warm. She surrounded Jake's cockhead with her lips, then glided up and down his long cock; then she swallowed Trey's thicker cock and took him in and out.

She remembered what it was like to hold both cocks in her mouth at the same time, and wanted that again. She lapped her tongue around the base of Trey's cockhead, then stretched her mouth to slide Jake's narrower cockhead inside, too. Both men, pressed tight together, filled her mouth. She squeezed them and sucked, stroking the hard shafts with her hand.

Having both of them inside her mouth thrilled her. She felt hot tingling between her legs, her sex longing for these same cocks. Could they both fit . . . there?

The thought made wetness flood from her opening. She pushed herself up and dragged the crotch of her thong to one side, then arched over them. She squeezed their cocks together and lowered herself to them. Jake's eyes widened as he realized what she was going to do. At the first pressure of the two cockheads against her slit, she moaned. They pressed against her wetness and she eased downward. Trey's hand wrapped around the cocks, holding them in place as she lowered onto them. The cockheads pushed inside a little, stretching her. Wider . . . and wider. They were hard . . . and big . . . and she wanted them thrusting inside.

She lowered a little more, but couldn't quite take them in. Maybe she'd tensed in her anticipation . . . or maybe they were just too big. But she wanted a cock inside her.

She moaned in frustration.

"It's okay, sweetheart," Jake said. "We can try again another time." Jake withdrew his cock from Trey's grasp and moved aside. "Right now, let me watch Trey fuck you."

Danielle glided down, swallowing Trey's thick hard cock inside her. She wrapped her arms around him, and, as he stood up, she curled her legs around him, too. He pressed her against the rock wall, a slight horizontal bulge in the rock acting as a ledge to take some of her weight, and he surged forward. The fullness of his cock inside her sent her senses reeling. She wanted more.

He drew back and thrust again.

"Oh God, you two are so sexy." Jake stroked his cock as he watched Trey fuck her against the wall.

Trey's cock glided in and out of her, sending wild sensations dancing through her as he thrust deep. She squeezed him inside as she clung to his broad, muscular shoulders. Such strength. Such raw male power.

His cock drove deep again, then again. Intense pleasure bubbled up, then exploded in a mind-shattering orgasm as she wailed her release.

They clung to each other, breathing heavily in the aftermath. Finally, he lowered her to her feet and guided her back to the blanket. She lay down and Jake settled beside her. He grasped her T-shirt—she'd forgotten she still wore it—and drew it over her head, then tossed it aside. Next, he pulled away her thong, which had merely been pushed aside to accommodate Trey's cock sliding into her.

He knelt over her. His warm hands found her breasts and he warmed them in his big palms. She grasped his cock, hard and twitching, then drew it toward her mouth. When she swallowed him inside again, he groaned. She sucked and licked, watching his blue eyes darken to navy.

He drew away from her, then lowered himself until his cock pressed against her wet opening.

"Fuck me, Jake."

He drove inside, then kept on driving until she was gasping with need.

"Oh, yeah . . . oh, Jake . . ."

"Come for me, sweetie. Let me hear you come."

"Yes, I'm . . ." Pleasure tumbled through her, then shot off the scale. "I'm coming." She gasped, then moaned as her cells tightened, then exploded in intense, vibrant bliss.

She rode the wave of pleasure, Jake thrusting into her in a steady rhythm. Finally, he groaned and released inside her as she reached a pinnacle of pleasure.

As she clung to him, listening to her heartbeat slow to a more normal pace, she felt Trey lie down beside her. Jake shifted to her other side, and her two lovers held her between them, as the rain pitter-pattered outside in a soft, calm rhythm.

Danielle's lips released Jake's and she smiled at him, feeling a little misty. She'd already hugged and kissed Trey good-bye. Now it was time to go. She turned to grab her small suitcase to put it in the backseat of her car, but Trey already had it and stowed it away for her.

It had been a beautiful Sunday. Warm and bright with a blue cloudless sky. The three of them had started the morning with languorous lovemaking, then had a decadent brunch, followed by a dip in Jake's pool. Now the weekend was over.

Time to return to her regular life. Time to leave these two wonderful men behind.

She sighed and climbed into the driver's seat. It was hot inside the car. She turned the key in the ignition and the engine thrummed to life. She opened the windows and stared up at Trey and Jake standing beside the car in the driveway.

"Don't look so glum." Jake leaned on the door and smiled. "You're coming back next weekend, right?"

She nodded.

"My place next time," said Trey. "And I'll make dinner on Friday."

"It's a date." She smiled, then glanced in her rearview mirror. "I guess I'd better get going." What she really wanted to do was leap from the car and throw herself into Trey's arms . . . or Jake's . . . then drag them back into the house for another rousing round of lovemaking. . . . But she had to go home sometime.

The guys stepped back from the car and she pulled out of the driveway, then waved at them as she drove away.

Damn, but she hated to leave.

With them she felt happy and alive. At home she felt . . . lonely.

As she drove, she reminded herself how well the weekend had gone. Not only had she been well loved, but she felt that the men were opening up to each other, too. Jake clearly responded to Trey's touch . . . and Trey seemed to be open to more intimate interactions with Jake.

An hour and a half of driving later, she pulled up to her own house. As the week wore on, she threw herself into her work, but still felt the tug of her longing to be back in Carleton Falls. To be with Trey and Jake.

Finally, Friday came. She sped through her work, completing the Web site for her newest client, installing it, and ensuring it was fully functional. Then she packed up her things and tossed her suitcase in the backseat.

She could hardly wait to arrive at Trey's.

Nine

Danielle pulled into Trey's driveway, beside the torch red Mustang. Jake's car. He was already here. The two of them were waiting for her.

She grabbed her bag from the backseat and raced for the door, then rang the doorbell. She waited impatiently for the door to open, wanting to throw herself into Trey's arms—or Jake's—as soon as the door opened.

She heard the click of the lock, and then the heavy oak door opened. Trey stood in front of her looking incredibly sexy wearing . . . well, very little. He wore a white shirt collar with a small bow tie, and shirt cuffs . . . but no shirt. Just a broad expanse of well-toned muscular chest and bulging arms. Slim-fitting black pants covered his lower body. Clearly, he was dressed to be her manservant . . . and she licked her lips as thoughts of exactly how she might make use of his services swirled through her mind.

"Mistress Rayne. Welcome." Trey bowed, then stepped back to allow her to come inside.

Jake stepped into the room, wearing the same outfit, carrying a tall stemmed glass of white wine. He handed it to her while Trey took her bag down the hall, probably to the bedroom.

"Would you like to come into the kitchen while we prepare the meal?" Jake asked.

"Certainly," she responded, falling into the role.

Jake led her through the kitchen door into Trey's wonderfully large, bright kitchen with its light-stained wooden cabinets, white tiled countertops, and white appliances. Such a difference from Jake's kitchen with its elegant dark-stained cherry cabinets, black marble countertops, and stainless-steel appliances.

A platter sat on the counter with large pink shrimp and bright yellow lemon wedges on crushed ice, a bowl of red sauce in the center. Beside that stood a gray marble tray with a variety of cheeses and fancy crackers and another platter with fresh-cut vegetables and dip.

"Would you like to sit at the table or the counter?" Trey asked.

Like in Jake's kitchen, Trey had a sitting area at the counter with tall stools, but that's where the similarity ended. Jake's house was all streamlined elegance whereas Trey's house had a homier, more casual feel. Trey's living room had cozy cloth couches and carpet whereas Jake's had tailored leather and dark oak hardwood.

She glanced toward the round table in the breakfast nook surrounded by windows and facing the large backyard, kept private by a tall hedge surrounding the property.

"I think I'll stay by the counter. Close to the food."

Jake pulled out one of the high stools under the counter bar and she sat down. He turned and stepped toward the white oven. She watched his lovely tight butt as he leaned over to check whatever was cooking inside the oven. She sipped her wine, enjoying the delicate, slightly fruity flavor. Trey returned and smiled her way.

"Is there anything I can get you, mistress?"

Mistress. Mmm. That had a delightful ring to it. In fact, it sent thrills through her as she imagined both men following some very interesting commands.

She wanted to order him to kiss her, then strip off her clothes, or his . . . or maybe Jake's . . . but she didn't want to speed things along too much. Especially since they'd gone to a lot of trouble to prepare a lovely meal.

"I'd like a shrimp."

The platter was right in front of her, but she smiled at him rather than reaching for one.

"Of course, mistress." Trey lifted one of the lemon wedges lying on the ice and squeezed it onto a plump shrimp, which he then dipped in the red sauce. He brought the juicy morsel to her lips.

She opened and he slipped the end of the shrimp into her mouth. She bit off a piece, and lemon juice dribbled down her chin as she chewed. Trey stroked his finger along her chin, gathering the juice on his fingertip, then held it to her lips. She opened her mouth, then lapped at his finger. She grasped his hand and drew his finger deeper into her mouth, sucking lightly . . . then released him.

"Would mistress like some celery?" he asked, his chocolate brown eyes simmering.

She nodded, and opened her mouth. He fed her a small green stick with dip. A few moments later, Jake joined them, and the two of them alternated feeding her. Soon she found herself filling up on veggies and shrimp, while starving for the taste of male flesh.

A timer went off and Trey opened the oven and brought out a big flat pan. A wonderful aroma filled the room as he transferred the contents onto a platter and set it on the countertop. It had an attractive display of items, such as glazed chicken chunks on skewers, bacon-wrapped scallops, and little triangles of stuffed phyllo pastry. From the delicious aroma, with a hint of cinnamon, she suspected the latter were filled with spiced beef.

"They smell wonderful," she said.

Jake picked up one of the scallops and fed it to her.

"Mmm." She picked up a pastry and held it toward him. "Time for you to try."

He took a bite, careful not to burn himself on the contents, chewed, then licked his lips. She watched his tongue outline his mouth, longing to do the same with her own tongue. He leaned forward and nibbled the rest of the pastry from her fingers, then nipped her fingertips. She felt her finger pulled into his mouth, and he sucked lightly. The feel of his warm mouth surrounding her sent heat thrumming through her body.

Trey offered her a chunk of chicken from a skewer, then popped a piece into his own mouth. She watched the sensual movement of his lips as he chewed. She grabbed another scallop and peeled off the bacon, then ate it slowly. Once done with the bacon, she offered the scallop to Trey. He leaned forward and opened his mouth. She fed in only half, then leaned forward to capture the other half in her mouth. Their lips met and she kissed him. Only their mouths touched, nothing else, but the feel of his masculine lips moving sensually against hers sent her hormones blazing.

"As delicious as this is, I've had enough food for now." She stood up with her glass of wine in hand and moved into the living room.

Trey and Jake followed, Jake carrying a bottle of wine and Trey two glasses. She sat down on the couch, sinking into the comfy cushions, hoping the men would join her, but instead, Trey slid an ottoman in front of her and lifted her legs onto it. Both men knelt down in front of her. Each took one of her feet in his hands, then began massaging. She sighed at the exquisite decadence of it all.

The gentle pressure of theirs hands as they stroked and squeezed her feet made her tingle all over. After a nice long relaxing massage, Trey's hands began to move up her calf. Jake followed suit. They stroked and rubbed, then moved up even more. Her thighs tingled in appreciation and her insides throbbed in anticipation. Soon, they were sliding her skirt upward, and their big, masculine hands stroked closer to her melting heat . . . then closer . . .

Trey's fingers found her first, then stroked over her mound. Jake grasped the elastic on her undies and pulled them downward as Trey drew the ottoman away. Jake knelt in front of her and drew her legs apart, settling them over his shoulders. Then she felt him touch her. First with his fingers, stroking her wet opening, then sliding inside her. She sighed at the erotic invasion. Then his mouth touched her and she moaned. His tongue dipped inside and he swirled it around, then covered her clit. As she gasped, she arched her back.

While Jake was busy down below, Trey unfastened the first button of her blouse and kissed her chest, moving downward as he released button after button. Jake leaned back and watched Trey unfasten her bra and peel it from her breasts. Both their gazes were steaming hot. Jake reached for one naked breast and stroked the hard nipple as Trey covered the other with his hot wet mouth. Jake licked her clit again and she moaned. So many sensations dazzling her senses . . . she could barely . . .

Oh, Jake's tongue tortured her clit. Trey sucked on her hard nipple. She felt herself accelerating toward rapturous release. Heat building . . . senses reeling . . .

Jake sucked on her clit as he swirled his finger inside her.

Heat singed her senses as it exploded through her. She wailed in a fast and furious orgasm, waves of pleasure wafting through her.

Finally, she fell back on the couch, spent.

She was a mess of disheveled clothing. Her bra lay tossed across her throat, her blouse flopped open at her sides, and her skirt twisted around her waist. Trey helped her up and slid her blouse from her shoulders, then pulled away her bra. Jake drew her skirt down her legs and off. She sat back on the couch, totally naked, and smiled at them.

"Now I'd like you both to take off your pants."

She watched in anticipation as Trey pulled open his belt, then slowly lowered the zipper of his fly, revealing a glimpse of black-on-gray striped boxers. He dropped the black pants to the floor, giving her a great view of long muscular legs. Jake turned around and pivoted his tight butt from side to side, his light brown ponytail swishing across his back, then dropped his pants to the floor. The black briefs he wore accentuated the tight muscles of that glorious behind.

"Keep going, gentlemen," she instructed.

Trey grinned as he eased his boxers down. His thick cock stood upward curving toward his body.

Jake winked at her over his shoulder, then disposed of his briefs in a quick motion, revealing his hard muscular ass. Then he turned around. His long cock also stood tall and proud.

They looked incredible standing there, all hard male muscle, gloriously naked except for the collars and cuffs.

"Come here." She licked her lips as they approached.

They stood in front of her and she wrapped her hands around both cocks. Jake's hard member twitched in her hand. She stroked the length of Trey's shaft while she stroked the tip of Jake's. She tugged on Trey, drawing him closer, then licked his tip. Jake stepped closer, too, and she licked him, then took his cockhead into her mouth. She stroked her tongue around him and teased the tiny hole on the tip while she pumped Trey up and down. Then she switched, taking Trey in her mouth and pumping Jake.

They were rock hard . . . and close. If she kept either of them in her mouth much longer, they'd erupt. She stared at her handiwork, admiring the tall proud cocks as she held them, her fingers wrapped snugly around the hard shafts.

She released them and leaned back against the couch,

her hands behind her head. With them essentially following her orders, this was a perfect opportunity to have them interact with each other a little more.

"Trey, take Jake's cock and stroke it."

Trey turned to Jake and wrapped his hand around Jake's cock. As his hand moved, Jake's eyelids fell closed.

"Run you hand over his ass," she instructed.

Trey's free hand stroked over Jake's tight buttocks while his other hand stroked Jake's hard cock.

"Now take him in your mouth."

Trey raised an eyebrow at her, but he knelt down and turned Jake toward him, then brought the purple-faced cock to his mouth. He covered it with his lips, then swallowed it. Danielle watched in fascination as Jake's cock disappeared in and out of Trey's mouth as he pulsed up and down.

Danielle stroked Jake's firm stomach, then over his hip to his hard buttock. She caressed the hard-muscled flesh.

"Make him come for me, Trey."

Trey stroked Jake's other buttock as he sucked on his long hard cock. Up and down, pulsing and squeezing. Jake's face contorted in pleasure and he groaned. Danielle almost groaned herself, thinking of how good it would feel to have that hard cock inside her. Trey continued pumping and sucking, and finally, Jake stiffened and grunted, clearly finding his release.

"Very good. Now, Trey, come sit by me."

Trey gave Jake's cock one last lick, then stood up and sat down beside Danielle, his cock standing straight up in desperation for his own release.

"Now, Jake, come over here. Trey needs attention."

Jake knelt in front of Trey, giving Danielle a sidelong glance. He leaned forward and dove down on Trey's cock. Trey groaned. His head arched upward, his neck muscles taut. Danielle glided her fingers over Trey's small hard nipple as she watched Jake bob up and down. She stroked her fingers through Jake's hair, then tugged free the elastic binding it and stroked her fingers through the long, silky strands. Jake sucked and bobbed on Trey. She leaned over and licked Trey's nipple, then sucked on it. His hand wrapped around her head, his fingers forking through her hair.

Trey threw his head back and groaned. Jake continued to suck as Trey climaxed.

Danielle sat back on the couch and Jake glided up and down a few more times, then released Trey's cock from his mouth.

Jake smiled and turned to Danielle. "Now, mistress, what can we do to please you?" His gaze fell on her breasts, and she felt her nipples harden even more.

"Well, I think you two did such a good job, I think you deserve a kiss."

Jake smiled and reached for her but she shook her head.

"I mean you two."

Ten

Jake and Trey both glanced at Danielle, but she simply smiled. "Go on. Give each other a kiss."

Trey stood up and approached Jake. As their mouths drew close, excitement trembled through her. Jake stood stock still as their lips touched, but Trey reached for Jake and cupped his head, then deepened the kiss. Jake wrapped his arms around Trey and their kiss turned passionate. Danielle sighed. It was so romantic.

Then they parted and Trey whispered something in Jake's ear. An evil grin split his face and he nodded. Trey walked toward the hallway and disappeared.

"Hey, I thought you were supposed to follow my orders."

Jake took her hands and pulled her to her feet, then dragged her against his body. Her soft breasts crushed against his hard chest as he took her lips in a demanding kiss. His tongue sought hers, then curled against it in a passionate dance. She felt breathless and thoughts scattered from her brain. His hands roamed down her body, then cupped her ass as he pulled her tighter to him, his cock pressing tight against her belly.

A moment later, she felt Trey's hands on her shoulders, then his lips against her neck. Nuzzling. Sending tingles along her spine. Jake released her lips and kissed the other side of her neck.

"Aren't you going to—?" She gasped as Jake's mouth covered her nipple and he sucked. "Oh . . . I thought I was in charge. . . ."

Trey wrapped his hands around her arms and drew them behind her back, forcing her breasts forward. Jake feasted on one nipple, then the other.

"You were," Trey said. "Until you pushed too far. Then we decided to break free of our captivity"—he pulled her backward, and Jake grabbed her thighs and lifted her from the floor—"by making you *our* captive."

Excitement quivered through her as they carried her down the hall.

Their captive. Oh, this should be good.

They tossed her onto the big bed, which she noticed had been stripped of bedclothes except for the taupe sheet covering the thick mattress. Soft cloth cuffs dangled from the wooden posts of the headboard and footboard. Trey fastened her wrists in one set of cuffs while Jake fastened her ankles with the other.

She lay spread-eagled on the bed . . . totally naked. The men were naked, too, except for those cuffs, but she felt so . . . vulnerable. And she loved it.

Trey flicked off one cuff, then the other, then removed the collar. Jake followed suit.

"We are no longer your servants, mistress. Now we are your masters, and you are our slave." Trey stroked his finger down her chest . . . between her breasts . . . past her navel . . . then held still just above her curls. "If you agree to obey us, we'll untie you."

"I will not obey you," she said. 'Cause she sure didn't want them to untie her.

Jake leaned down and nibbled her knee, then kissed up her thigh . . . stopping just short of her slick aching flesh. Trey shifted beside her and turned her head to face him, then pressed his cock to her lips. He eased forward, and filled her mouth with the hot bulbous head. Jake sat on the other side of her. Trey pulled free of her mouth, then Jake turned her to him and pressed his cock into her mouth. After a couple of short thrusts, he drew back, and then they both pressed their cockheads to her lips and pressed them in a little. She licked them—she couldn't help herself—then opened wider to accommodate them. They pushed in a little more, filling her mouth. She squeezed them and sucked.

"Oh God, I want to feel our slave's warm pussy around me." Jake pulled free.

Trey pushed his cock deep into her mouth. She felt Jake prowl over her and then his hard cock nudge against her wet slit. Hard and sturdy, it pressed against her, sending her senses reeling . . . slowly opening her as it glided inside. She breathed in a rush of air as she sucked on Trey.

"Man, Trey, she is hot and tight."

Trey drew his cock from her mouth and sat on the side of the bed. Jake drew back and thrust forward. Trey wrapped his hand around his cock and stroked it as he watched Jake's cock glide into her again. Trey's free hand found her breast and stroked her hard sensitive nipple.

Jake pulled back and thrust again. She squeezed him inside her. His big cock stretched her as it glided along her slick passage. Trey sucked on her breast and Jake picked up speed. Thrusting deep and fast. She moaned at the exquisite pleasure of Trey's sucking and Jake's fucking.

"Oh, yes . . ."

Jake slowed and drew back, only his cockhead lingering in her needy opening.

"Oh, please keep going," she pleaded.

"So you've decided you want to obey your former servants, slave?"

She gasped as he almost pulled free. "Yes, I'll do anything you say." She arched forward, trying to keep him within her. "Just keep going," she cried frantically.

He impaled her with one forceful forward thrust. She moaned in delight.

Trey released her breast and sat back against the pillows, stroking his shaft. Jake began fucking her in earnest, driving deep, then pulling back . . . then driving deep again. She squeezed him inside, quivering pleasure trembling through her as he picked up speed . . . driving into her in forceful thrusts . . . sending her pleasure higher and higher . . . until she exploded in a spectacular release . . . flying across the heavens in pure rapture.

His groan joined hers as he burst into her . . . filling her with liquid heat.

"Man, it's my turn now."

Danielle, lying slumped back with her eyes closed . . . reveling in the afterglow of pleasure . . . felt the cuffs around one ankle pull free, then her legs lifted upright until they were pointing straight up, and then cuffed together. She opened her eyes to see Trey crouching against her, then his thick cock pushed into her.

Oh, it felt so good. His hard shaft filled the place Jake had just left . . . and stretched her even more with his wider cock. Then he grasped the cuffs between her ankles, and moved her feet to the left in a sweeping motion, then to the right. Her body twisted back and forth with the movement, essentially rolling her vagina around his cock. She squeezed him and he groaned. Jake slid his hand down her stomach and his finger glided over her clit. Within seconds

Trey erupted inside her. At the feel of his hot release, and Jake's stimulating touch, heat rushed through her and she moaned in another orgasm.

She stared at him wide-eyed while her breathing settled.

"What was that?" she asked.

"That . . . was spectacular," said Trey, smiling.

Jake held open the large wooden door and Danielle stepped into the dimly lit club. After lazing around Trey's place all morning, Trey had suggested they go to Le Jazz Hot, a local bar where he said they could listen to some great jazz music and do some dancing.

The hostess led them to a cozy booth in the corner with a great view of the stage. Small amber pendant shades hung from the ceiling over each of the tables, casting a soft glow.

The décor included glossy oak tables and comfy-looking black chairs with upholstered seats, wood paneling on most of the walls, and terra-cotta brick behind the stage area and the bar, and extending along a wall with a big fireplace. Over the bar a glittering array of stemmed glasses hung upside down, and inset shelves displayed bottles of liquor. The bar itself was made of stacked slate topped by a thick, glossy oak top. Various musical instruments were mounted on the walls, along with photos of famous jazz musicians. At least she assumed the latter, since she didn't know that much about jazz.

All in all the place had a nice warm feel. She sat down in the booth and Trey and Jake slid in beside her, one on each side. She ordered a glass of white wine and each of them ordered a beer.

"What do you think?" Trey asked.

"I like it," she answered.

"Wait till you hear the music."

The waitress brought their drinks and they settled back as the musicians took their places.

"This group plays jazz fusion," said Trey.

Danielle sipped her wine as she watched the men, wearing jeans and long-sleeved shirts, pick up their instruments.

"I've listened to a little jazz on the radio," she said, "but I don't know about the different styles."

"Well, jazz fusion doesn't get much broadcast time, probably because of its complexity, and the fact that it usually has no vocal . . . and the tracks are quite long, too." Trey sat back and smiled. "This should be a real treat for you."

The musicians began their set. Danielle snuggled against Jake as she enjoyed the raw energy of the music. She especially enjoyed the sweet sound of the saxophone. She could feel the sax player's sheer love of playing in the vitality and edginess of the music. When he ran down a flurry of notes, tingles ran down her spine; then when he switched to rich low notes, the deep tones raised the hairs on her arms.

Too soon the set was over.

Trey smiled at her, his eyebrow arching up.

Danielle nodded. "That was really something."

A DJ began to play a slow dance number.

"So, how about a dance?" Jake asked.

She sipped her wine, then followed him to the dance floor, where he slid his arms around her and held her close. She danced with him for a while, enjoying floating on a cloud of music with Jake guiding the way. After a while they returned to the table, and a few minutes later Trey asked her to dance. They danced to several slow songs. With his arms around her and his body close, she became intensely aware of her breasts pressed tight against him. The need built within her. She snuggled against him. It would be so nice to return to the house and get closer still.

Trey must have sensed her thoughts, because he leaned close to her ear and said, "You interested in heading back to my place?"

"Don't you want to catch another set?"

He nuzzled her ear. "I'd rather catch you."

Memories of being captured by him the night before flooded through her and heat rose within her.

She grabbed his hand. "Let's go." She turned and led him from the dance floor.

As they headed toward the table, she realized someone had joined Jake.

Jake seemed deep in conversation with the other man,

but he glanced up as Danielle and Trey approached. He seemed a little uncomfortable.

"Uh . . . Rico, these are my friends, Danielle and Trey."

The dark-haired young man turned toward them and glared. "Friends? Is that all?"

"Rico. That's enough." Jake's warning tone quieted the man.

"We were thinking of going back to my place," Trey said.

"Okay, uh . . ." He turned to Rico. "Wait here a minute."

He stood up and walked with them a few paces from the table. The other man sat at the table glowering.

"Look, he's had a few drinks and . . . I want to make sure he gets home okay. He's got his car here. I'm going to drive him."

"Sure, that's fine," Trey said. "You can meet up with us later."

Jake patted Trey on the shoulder. "Thanks, I'll do that." He sent Danielle a heated gaze. "I'll definitely do that."

She walked out the door with Trey, then to his car. "How will Jake get back to your place?"

"He'll probably take a cab. Or maybe he'll drive Rico's car. That'd serve Rico right if he woke up tomorrow and had no idea where he'd left it."

"Who is this Rico anyway?"

"He and Jake had a thing going, but it ended about six

months ago. I don't know a lot about it, but some friends Jake and I have in common told me that Rico wasn't very happy about it. He's the jealous type. That's a big reason Jake had to call it quits. It's tough when you're attracted to either men or women. . . . The guy suspected Jake of cheating whenever he spent any time with *anyone*. It became a real headache."

"So now they're broken up but this guy is still jealous?"

Trey shrugged. "Love is never simple."

Well, that sure was the truth.

Trey drove his car through the dark streets to his house, then pulled into the driveway. Hickory, Trey's cat, pranced across the front lawn and met them at the door, meowing and rubbing against his legs as he unlocked the door.

"Yeah, I get it. You want some dinner."

Danielle petted the sleek cat, but when the door opened, Hickory raced inside straight to the kitchen.

Danielle kicked off her shoes, and Trey helped her take off her sweater, then hung it up in the front closet. Hickory trotted back into the room, mewing loudly.

"I'll go feed Mr. Grumbles here. Why don't you get comfortable?"

She sat down on the couch as Trey disappeared into the kitchen. A moment later, she heard the can opener, followed by Hickory's frantic meowing. She picked up the remote control from the table and pressed the button to play music from Trey's playlist. He had shown her yesterday how he had his entertainment computer, as he called it, set up to record from the TV, to play music, et cetera. A soft, jazzy piece, primarily piano, filled the room, and she relaxed against the cushions.

"I thought you were going to make yourself comfortable." Trey grinned as he settled beside her. He drew her close and kissed her, his lips lingering while his hands slid from her shoulders to the front of her blouse. He released the first button, then the second. Her skin tingled as his fingertips brushed her skin, gliding over the swell of her breasts above the lace of her bra.

"Aren't we going to wait for Jake?"

The tangy scent of his cologne and the light shadowing across his jaw proved irresistible, and she caressed his cheek, loving the bristly, masculine feel of his whiskers.

He grasped her hand and kissed it. "I should go shave."

"No, don't. It's sexy."

His eyes glinted. "You say that now, but when I kiss you . . . where I intend to kiss you . . . you might not be so happy with the reality of sandpaper against your skin."

"Well . . ." She leaned forward and nibbled his chin, dragging her teeth along the bristles, enjoying the raspy sound. She nuzzled his neck, kissing the pulse at the base. "If you insist."

He kissed her again, then stood up and headed down the hall. As he closed the bathroom door, Hickory trotted toward the couch.

"Hey, there. All finished with dinner?"

He mewed and leapt onto the couch, then climbed onto her leg and mewed again, staring at her with big amber eyes. She stroked his head. He flopped down on her lap, clearly settling in for a long petting session. The soft feel of his fur under her hand and the quiet rumble of his purring delighted her. Maybe she should get a cat.

The phone rang. Hickory's ears perked up and she gazed down at him.

"That's probably Jake."

Eleven

The phone rang again and Danielle glanced around. One of the cordless phones sat in its charging unit beside the computer. She cuddled Hickory against her, his fur soft against her bare chest, and stroked him as she crossed the room to pick up the phone.

"Hello?"

"Hi there. Who's this?" a woman's voice said.

If she'd been at home, Danielle would have asked who the woman was rather than answering, but she was a guest at Trey's, and it was natural that the caller might wonder who was answering Trey's phone.

"This is Danielle, a friend of Trey's. May I ask who's calling?"

"Hi. I'm Suzie. Where's Trey?"

"He's busy at the moment. May I have him call you back? He'll be only a few minutes."

Hickory murmured, then wriggled in her arms. She set him on the floor and he bounded away.

"So how do you know Trey?" the caller asked.

"I . . . uh . . . I'm a friend of his from college." She didn't know who this woman was or why she should be answering her questions.

"Oh. Are you visiting from out of town?"

Danielle wasn't used to being badgered for answers and didn't really know how to handle it. She didn't want to answer this inquisitive unknown woman's questions but wasn't quite sure how to avoid it, other than just holding her silence . . . or hanging up. Both seemed rude. It was just easier to answer.

"Yes, I am."

"Do you know Jake, too?"

"Uh . . . yes." Had this woman known Trey for a long time? The thought sent a pang of jealousy through her . . . which was ridiculous. Danielle didn't have any designs on Trey. She wanted Jake and Trey to wind up together. Enjoying the journey was simply a bonus.

"Jake's a great guy, isn't he?"

Was that a subtle hint? Danielle wondered. In other words, was she saying *Keep your hands off my man.*

"Where do you live, Danielle?"

"I live in Phoenicia."

"Is that a long way from Carleton Falls?"

So the woman didn't live in Carleton Falls; otherwise she'd know where Phoenicia was.

Trey walked into the room.

"Um . . . Trey's back. I'll put him on."

She handed the phone to Trey. "It's someone named Suzie."

Immediately, Trey's face lit up. He took the phone.

"Hey, Suzie, how are you?"

His broad smile and glittering eyes told her this Suzie was someone very special to him. Again, jealousy niggled through her.

"Yes . . . Danielle. Yes . . . she's a friend."

Not a girlfriend. Of course she wasn't, but at that moment she wished she were.

Shock catapulted through her.

Damn it. She wasn't supposed to feel that way. Jake would be heartbroken.

Trey wandered into the kitchen and his voice became a low mumble through the door.

Curiosity zinged through Danielle. Who was this Suzie woman?

A few minutes later, Trey stepped back into the room, sipping a glass of ice water.

"Yes, honey. Okay." He placed the glass on the table and sat beside Danielle on the couch. "Sure, we can talk tomorrow." He winked at Danielle. "Okay. Yes, I love you, too." He pressed the End button and set the phone on the table.

He turned to Danielle and slid his arms around her. "Now . . . where were we?"

She remained stiff in his arms. "You are kidding, right?"

His brown eyes narrowed in puzzlement. "Is something wrong?"

"You mean besides the fact that you just told a woman you love her . . . right before you try to make out with me?"

He chuckled. "You don't think . . ." At her stony stare, he laughed again. "That was my little sister, Suzie."

"Your sister?"

"That's right."

Relief surged through her as he pulled her against him and nuzzled her cheek. "So, what, you think I'm the type of guy to have a harem of women at my beck and call? That I keep them on a string, telling them I love them so I can entice them into my bed whenever I want?"

She jabbed his chest, embarrassment coursing through her. "Oh, shut up."

She fastened her mouth on his to stop his laughter. His lips played on hers, but when her tongue slid between his lips, he drew her tight against him and answered her invitation with a swirl of his tongue. Then he leaned her back against the cushions and kissed down her neck, then nuzzled between her breasts.

She hadn't even refastened her blouse buttons. The whole time she'd been talking to Trey's little sister, her breasts had been hanging out. Her cheeks flushed, which was ridiculous, since the woman hadn't been able to see her . . . but Danielle still felt embarrassed. What was happening to her? She'd never been so consumed by a relationship before—and it wasn't even like this was a real relationship. Was it?

But as Trey drew her bra cup down and nuzzled the swell of her breast, all thoughts fled her mind. All she could concentrate on was Trey's lips caressing her skin, sending tingles through her, closing in on her nipple. Then he covered it and she moaned. His tongue dabbed at the hard nub and then he sucked a little. Desire lanced through her. She forked her fingers through his short sandy hair, drawing his head tighter against her. He lapped at her nipple, then kissed across her chest to her other needy nub.

She dragged her hand down his hard chest, to his stomach. She stroked over his rigid abs, then lower, to another rigid body part. As he licked and nibbled her nipple, she dragged his zipper down and slipped her hand inside. Her fingers wrapped around his long member, still covered with the soft cotton of his boxers.

He sucked her nipple and heat shot through her. She squeezed his long thick cock, then slid her fingers inside his boxers and stroked the hot silky skin stretched across his rock-hard shaft.

He kissed the base of her neck as he pushed her blouse from her shoulders.

"You have too many clothes on, woman," he said as his hands glided around her back and unfastened her bra.

"So do you," she responded as she squeezed his cock.

He stood up and shoved his pants and boxers out of the way in one movement. She slid her bra from her arms and tossed it aside, then shimmied out of her skirt. He unfastened his shirt and tossed it aside, then knelt in front of her, his brown eyes glittering as he watched her hook her thumbs under the elastic of her thong.

"Let me deal with these." He ran his finger along the crotch of her panties.

His touch, just a whisper from her slick flesh, sent her heart rate accelerating. He stroked down her thigh, then wrapped his hand around her calf and lifted her leg. He nuzzled her ankle, then kissed it, sending heat thrumming through her. He lifted her other leg and kissed behind her knee, then rested her legs over his shoulders. He grinned as he prowled forward and leaned in to her body. He kissed her stomach above the elastic of her thong . . . then grasped the elastic in his teeth. He drew it downward . . . slowly . . . revealing her auburn curls a little at a time.

God, she wanted to twine her fingers in his hair and drag him tight against her. To mash his face into her hot, slick flesh, to— Oh! His tongue dove into her and stroked her clit. Her heart thundered in her chest as she gasped.

His fingers hooked under the elastic and he dragged the small garment down her legs and tossed it aside. He lifted one of her legs again and kissed along the calf, then shifted to the other thigh. Her sex burned with need as his lips moved upward. He rested her legs over his shoulders again . . . then grinned at her. Or rather, at her . . . uh . . . pussy. His gaze, filled with intense male interest, burned through her. He continued his perusal, simply looking at her, and she squirmed a little.

He chuckled, then stroked her auburn curls with his fingertips in a gentle petting motion, then pressed his mouth to her and . . . The hot, sensual feel of his mouth kissing and nibbling her wet flesh sent dizzying sensations swirling through her. She curled her fingers through his short hair, needing to hang on to something. Her head dropped back on the couch and she moaned in desperate need as his tongue teased her throbbing clit. Her pulse pounded in her veins. He lapped, then sucked, and sparks flared inside her. He flicked his tongue, then sucked again, and intense heat swelled through her, sending her senses reeling. Pleasure rocketed through her and she moaned as release came fast and furious.

Still he sucked and licked.

She tugged on him. "I want you inside me, Trey."

He prowled higher and rested his thick cock against her. She sighed as his hard flesh eased inside her, then she wrapped her legs around him and tried to pull him in further.

"Deeper," she insisted.

He thrust forward and she moaned at the incredible invasion of hard flesh. She squeezed him, feeling his thick shaft inside her, gliding forward, then drawing back.

"Yes, Trey. Harder."

He thrust and thrust again. His cock went impossibly deep as he drove forward, lifting her legs high and wide.

"Oh, God—!" An incredible orgasm blossomed through her and her limbs melted into useless flesh.

Trey kept on thrusting as wave after wave of pleasure flooded through her. He drove forward with a guttural groan and held, his cock pulsing, liquid heat filling her.

A moment later, he collapsed on top of her. She welcomed his weight, holding him tight to her. They stayed like that for quite a while. Danielle enjoyed the warmth and intimacy of their joined bodies . . . and the comfort of being in someone else's arms.

In Trey's arms.

Finally, Trey drew away. He smiled, then kissed her. As he slipped free of her body, she felt a sudden sense of loss. It was so comforting sharing that intimacy with him. Feeling so close to him.

Then suddenly she realized just how intimate this felt . . . with just the two of them here. Like two actual lovers. Two lovers in a relationship.

Heat drained from her face as she realized she'd been playing a dangerous game. She'd been having casual sex with her two friends, having fun and hoping to play matchmaker . . . but along the way, she was in danger of losing her own heart.

"What's wrong, sweetheart? You just went white as a ghost."

His charming smile along with the concern in his warm brown eyes made her feel loved. But she knew it wasn't love. At least, not romantic love. It was the caring of one friend for another. Very intimate friends.

She enjoyed getting close to them, but she had to make sure she didn't blow this whole thing out of proportion. She could have sex with Trey and Jake. It didn't mean anything deeper than three close friends sharing some intimate time. The thought of being in some kind of long-term relationship with two men—two men with a long history together and a host of unresolved issues—was simply ludicrous.

"I'm fine. I was just wondering what happened to Jake."

"Danielle?"

Danielle clung to sleep, despite the voice curling through her consciousness.

"Danielle? Wake up, sleepyhead."

Warm lips caressing her neck sent tingles through her. She opened her eyes, murmuring soft sounds of approval.

Trey gazed at her and smiled. "Hey there. We need to get a move on if we're going to go windsurfing today."

She reached for him and drew him forward. He gave her a brief kiss, then stroked her hair behind her ears.

"Come on, sweetheart. It's time to get up."

"Mmm. Time to come back to bed." She wanted to snuggle against his warm, masculine body again.

He grinned, but drew back, tugging on her hands. "Tempting, but you assured me last night that you wanted to try windsurfing again, and if we don't get there soon, the boards will all be rented."

She closed her eyes again. "Windsurfing is nice, but bed is nicer."

Bright light shone on her face and she grumbled and opened her eyes again, shielding them with her hand. Trey had opened the blinds and allowed the sunshine to blaze in the window.

"It's a beautiful day outside. It's supposed to hit eighty degrees and the wind will be about seven knots. It's the perfect day."

"Okay, okay," she grumbled as she pushed the bed-clothes aside and sat up. Hickory grumbled from the end of the bed, then leapt to the floor and stalked off.

"You aren't really a morning person, are you?" he teased, then wrapped his arms around her and kissed her silly.

"Well, when you start my morning with a kiss like

that . . ." She stroked her fingers through his hair, then captured his mouth again for a lingering kiss.

He drew away and chuckled. "Oh no you don't." He took her hands and drew her forward. "We need to get going. How long will it take you to throw on a bathing suit and shorts?"

"All right already. You're really worried about no boards?"

"If we're not there in"—he glanced at his wristwatch—"say forty minutes, I'd say we lose."

"Okay. Five minutes."

Danielle unzipped her suitcase, sitting on the dresser, and rifled through it for her bathing suit. Seven minutes later, they stepped out into the bright sunshine. A warm breeze caressed her cheek. Trey opened the car door for her, then handed her a travel mug full of an aromatic vanilla coffee blend. As he got into the driver's seat, she sipped then placed the mug in the cup holder beside her seat.

"What about Jake?" she asked. "He wanted to come, too, didn't he? Do you think something happened to him last night that stopped him from showing up?"

"No, he knew when we'd planned to go so he'll probably assume we're still picking him up." Trey handed her his cell phone. "Do you want to give him a call to let him know we're on our way?"

She took the small sleek phone and pressed the On

button, but nothing happened. She tried again. "I think your battery needs charging."

"Damn. Well, we'll be there in a couple of minutes."

Ten minutes later, they pulled up in front of Jake's charming brick two-story house. Trey opened her door and offered a hand to help her from the car, and they walked up the stone path through Jake's bright-colored garden to his front door.

Trey rang the doorbell. The inside door opened, and Rico, naked except for a navy towel draped carelessly around his waist, glared at them through the glass of the storm door.

"Yes?"

"Uh . . . is Jake in?" Danielle asked.

"Yes. He's in the shower right now." He grinned wickedly. "And I'm just about to join him. I'll tell him you came by." With that, he shoved the door closed in their faces.

Danielle blinked, then stared at Trey. His closed expression gave nothing away.

Jake had started up with Rico again? The guy certainly was good-looking but . . . with Rico's jealousy . . . Jake must know that it would put an end to what she and Trey and Jake had going. An end to any hope of getting back with Trey . . . at least for now.

Well, what could she expect? She had pushed this

whole thing on Jake. Maybe he hadn't wanted to be a part of it from the beginning. Maybe he feared Trey would never want to continue the relationship. Maybe seeing Rico's continued longing for him had boosted his spirits and made him want to be with someone who wanted him . . . not someone avoiding anything deeper, like Trey.

But she had seen the change in Trey. Surely Jake had, too. If only he'd given it a bit more time.

Sadness careened through her. If Jake was seeing Rico now . . . it meant the end of their relationship. But *she* still wanted to be with Jake.

She mentally shook herself. What the hell was she thinking? She was doing all this so that Trey and Jake could be together. Not for herself. Of course, she enjoyed the sex with them . . . the way they made her feel wanted . . . *the way they made her feel loved* . . .

Oh God, had she really let this become about her? How could she expect to build a relationship when she was seeing two men at once . . . at the same time? Was she really doing this because she hoped something would develop between her and Jake? Or her and Trey?

Oh, damn, her feelings were so mixed up. Of course she'd love to be loved by either one of these special men . . . but they belonged together. She could just tell. Even if Trey denied it to himself . . .

She glanced at Trey, who had led her back to the car.

"Danielle, don't let it bother you."

"What?" She gazed up at him as he held her car door open.

"Jake and Rico. Don't let it bother you. Even if he's decided to start up with Rico again . . . which means he won't be sharing with us . . . *I* still want you to keep coming around."

He swept her into his arms and kissed her, deeply and passionately.

"I don't want to lose you yet," he murmured against her lips, then kissed her again.

Twelve

Danielle drew her lips from Trey's, getting the sense that his mind was far away.

"Trey, what about you? Does it bother you that Jake might be seeing Rico again?"

"No, of course not," he said with a little too much conviction.

"Are you sure?"

He locked gazes with her. "Why should it? I mean, he can do whatever he wants. It's not like I have any claim to him."

Despite his words, she could see turmoil in his brown eyes.

"I just think that . . . maybe you still have feelings for Jake. You did have something special with him. At least I thought it was special."

Trey sighed. "That's true, but . . . it was a long time ago."

"But if you still have feelings for him . . . why couldn't you continue what you had before?"

His gaze sharpened. "Who said I still have feelings for him?"

She stroked his cheek. "I think there's still something between you. I think the two of you could—"

He grasped her arms. "Look, Danielle. Jake and I did have something special back in college, but it didn't work out. Okay?"

How could she argue with the denial in his eyes, even though she was sure in his heart, he felt differently?

Jake tied his robe and stepped into the living room. It was later than he'd thought. He and Trey and Danielle had plans today and damn Rico hadn't left yet. He'd already caused Jake enough inconvenience. Jake didn't intend to lose his Sunday with his friends.

Of course, the thought of Danielle's soft body pressed against his, his cock buried inside her, Trey on the other side of her . . . sent blood flooding to his groin. More than friends. A relationship he didn't want to lose anytime soon.

Rico stood at the window, staring out through the partially open horizontal blinds. "Ah, you should see your friends."

"My friends?" If Trey and Danielle had arrived, they

might misinterpret Rico's being here. He glanced out the window and saw Danielle and Trey in a passionate embrace. The sight sent a confusing surge of jealousy through him.

"It seems they're more interested in each other than in you," Rico said.

As Jake watched, Trey opened the door and he and Danielle stood talking intently. A moment later, Danielle got into the car.

"What the hell? Why are they leaving?"

"I don't know. I just told them you were in the shower."

Jake's gaze took in the towel loosely wrapped around Rico's narrow waist, and could just imagine the conversation.

"You led them to believe we're together again."

Rico didn't flinch, but Jake knew him well enough.

Damn, things were tenuous enough as it was with Trey. And Danielle . . . He did not want to lose her.

He glared at Rico. "Get the hell out of here. Now!"

He strode to the door and opened it, then yelled to Trey as he was getting in the car. "Trey! Wait!"

He slammed the door behind him and strode across his front lawn, wearing only his blue terry robe.

Danielle glanced around at Jake's voice. She stepped out of the car, and she and Trey walked toward Jake.

"Sorry I'm not quite ready. I guess you're wondering what Rico is doing here."

Opal Carew

"You don't need to explain, Jake," Danielle responded.

"I know. It's just that it's not what it appears. Rico moved recently, and when I went to drive him home last night, he wouldn't tell me his new address. I couldn't just dump him in the street, so I brought him back here. He slept in the guest room . . . and I'm not idiot enough to start up with him again. He's just too . . . emotional."

Relief swept through her. So she hadn't lost Jake yet.

The garage door opened, and a moment later a sporty black car backed out of the driveway and sped away with a squeal of tires, Rico's hand with a single-finger salute stuck out the window at them.

Trey grinned, and they all began to laugh.

Jake shook his head. "I'm not sure what I saw in him in the first place."

"Well, a great physique and exotic good looks for one," Trey answered.

Jake grinned. "Yeah, I guess. Great technique in bed and a nine-inch cock aren't bad reasons, either."

Danielle glanced from Jake to Trey and back again and grinned. "Certainly reasons I find quite convincing."

Jake wrapped his arms around her and pulled her close. "You're bad, sweetheart. Real bad."

She slid her hand discreetly under his robe and stroked his free-wheeling cock. It rose at her touch. "Of course I am. That's why you both love being with me so much."

"Nine inches, eh?" Trey stroked her shoulders. "Does that mean you like Jake better than me?"

Danielle chuckled. "You may not have the same length, but you know what to do with it." And, of course, he was thicker. Her hand itched to stroke him, too.

She released Jake's cock and stepped away. He smoothed down his robe.

"So you won't be choosing between us anytime soon?" Jake asked.

"Not if I don't have to."

Of course, she knew it wouldn't be a matter of her choosing. They would choose each other. It was as simple as that.

Danielle unfastened her shorts and pushed them off, then folded them and placed them in her beach bag. Jake removed his shirt and rolled it up, then set it on the picnic table they'd set their cooler on. Sunlight glittered on the water, and several windsurfers skimmed across the surface. One sailor swung his bright-colored sail around, sending his board curving in a new direction. Danielle watched as a young woman stepped from the dock onto her board and took off on the wind. Her companion followed suit, and a moment later they were in the middle of the bay sailing side by side.

"Trey seems to have had some luck," Jake said.

She glanced across the beach to the grassy peninsula where the rental stand was and saw Trey heading back toward them, a smile on his handsome tanned face. The breeze rippled through his short spiky hair, the sunlight accentuating the blond highlights in the sandy-colored mass.

When they'd arrived and seen the parking lot full and the crowd at the rental booth, they'd resigned themselves to the possibility that they wouldn't be windsurfing today. Trey had gotten in line while Jake and Danielle gathered their things and took them to the beach to claim a picnic table.

"I got two boards," Trey said, holding up two slips of paper.

"Only two?" Jake asked.

"I figure we'll take turns showing Danielle how to use the board."

Jake turned to Danielle. "I thought you already knew how to windsurf. We taught you before you moved to Boston."

"That was a long time ago. I haven't been on a board since."

"Let's fix that." Trey reached for her hand.

She placed her hand in his larger one, enjoying the feel of his large fingers wrapping around hers.

"Don't forget your water shoes."

She pulled the blue rubber shoes Trey had brought for her from her bag, knowing they were a wise precaution against getting cut by the sharp clam shells on the sandy bottom of the lake. Why he had a pair of ladies' size 7 shoes on hand, she didn't know . . . and didn't ask. The tug of his hand drew her forward as he crossed the sand to the grass, then toward the shore.

"That's us. Numbers five and twenty-seven," he said, gesturing to two windsurfing boards lying on the grass by the water's edge. "The last two."

Number 5 had a bright blue-and-green sail, while 27's sail was purple with bands of turquoise and hot pink.

She gravitated to 27.

"I knew you'd like that one." Trey pushed the board into the water.

Danielle sat on the grass and dropped the shoes into the water, then dipped her feet in. Goose bumps rose along her legs. "It's cold." She tugged on one shoe, then the other.

"It'll be fine once you're used to it." Jake pulled on his shoes, then stood up and waded into the water, guiding number 5 ahead of him. When he was thigh deep, he sat on the board, then pushed himself to his feet. He grabbed the boom of his sail, then drew it upward. He tipped the slack sail until the wind caught it, and deftly sailed away.

Trey pushed number 27 into the water. "Here, climb on."

She sat on the board and drew her legs onto it, then knelt as Trey guided the board deeper into the lake.

"Hang on." He grasped the board, then hopped onto it.

She hung on to the sides as it rocked, then he stood up and the board stabilized. Slowly, she stood up in front of him.

"Pick up the sail," he instructed.

Cautiously, she leaned down and grasped the boom, then lifted it slowly, keeping her weight carefully balanced on the board. Trey grasped the boom, too, his muscular arms around her, his hands right beside hers.

"Like this. Remember?"

He shifted the boom until the wind filled the sail, and then the board began to move . . . slowly, at first, then picking up speed. A tangle of memories wafted through her brain. Of Trey on the board behind her just like this. Of his body pressed against hers. His closeness sent her off balance. . . . Not physically. Physically, he kept her stable and skimming across the water quite nicely. Her emotions, however, somersaulted through her in wild disarray.

She'd wanted him so much that last summer. It had been building all year, and when he'd taken her on the board . . . when his body had been so close . . . his breath brushing across her nape . . . she'd almost died from yearning. But he belonged with Jake. And for the first time, she admitted to herself that Jake and Trey were one of the reasons she'd switched schools all those years ago.

And now, here she was in the exact same situation again.

As she leaned into Trey's body, she realized she wanted him to want her.

Well, he did *want* her. The bulge against the back of her bathing suit told her that. . . . But she wanted to be . . . special. That one person he'd want to spend a lifetime with. Which was crazy, especially since she realized she felt exactly the same way about Jake.

How could she want both men to want her as his one and only?

Especially since her whole mission was to bring the two of them together.

Obviously, she had these feelings because the two had been paying attention to her. Treating her special. But that was because they were her friends, not because they planned to forge a lifetime partnership.

Now that she'd finally opened herself to these men, it only made her realize how badly she wanted a lifetime companion . . . someone who would love her forever . . . stay with her forever . . . and that was causing her to jump at anyone who showed her any attention. How pathetic was that?

She had to keep things in perspective.

Trey's fingers slid over hers as he guided her to shift the boom and the board began to turn. She shifted her weight on her feet to balance as the board tipped into the turn, then straightened out under Trey's guidance.

"You know, I loved it when we used to come out here and windsurf together. Especially when I was teaching you." His lips nuzzled her neck, sending tingles down her spine. "In fact, you caused me some serious thinking."

"Really? Why?"

"Because . . . you used to do this"—he pressed his groin, and the large bulge in his trunks, against her back—"to me. Which caused me quite a bit of confusion, since I thought I was only attracted to men. Yet, all I had to do was get close to you to get this reaction from my body."

"You mean you were . . . attracted to me back then?" He had told her he and Jake had wondered about making love to her, but she hadn't thought it had been an actual physical attraction.

He chuckled. "That's an understatement."

"I hope I didn't . . . I mean, you and Jake . . . it didn't cause any problems, did it?"

Oh God, could she be the reason they broke up?

"Not exactly problems. In fact, after a day of wind-surfing with you, Jake and I would have the best sex ever. I talked to him about it, though. Discussed my confusion. He was very understanding."

"He didn't get mad . . . or hurt?"

"I don't think so. It's not like I acted on that attraction. And you had the same affect on him."

As their board approached a clump of other wind-surfers crossing in front of them, he guided the boom around so they changed direction again. "He'd been with women before. He knew he was attracted to both sexes. He also knew I'd never been attracted to a woman before. He was quite willing to talk to me about it."

"That must have been hard."

"I wasn't quite sure how to deal with it. I still wanted to make it work with Jake, even though deep inside I think we both realized then that what we had wouldn't last forever."

Her heart compressed at those words. Why couldn't it last forever? But that was long ago, she reminded herself. Maybe Trey had needed to explore . . . to test his desires and be with other people. But that didn't mean he couldn't find happiness now with Jake.

As they leaned a little to stabilize the board after bouncing over another board's wake, Trey's arm brushed along hers.

Did it have to be Jake, though? If Trey had been attracted to her then—she'd been the first woman he'd ever been attracted to!—then maybe . . . could she have a chance at happily-ever-after with Trey?

Her stomach churned. How could she even think such a thing? She knew how Jake cared for Trey.

"I did decide I needed to put some distance between you and me, though. You were leaving anyway, but that's why Jake took over your lessons."

She had felt it . . . Trey's withdrawal back then. She

had felt it as a coldness . . . him releasing their friendship . . . ready to move on. Those feelings were blown out
of proportion . . . she knew that now . . . but at the time,
she'd been vulnerable . . . leaving for a new place . . . having to start developing friendships over again. If they
could be put aside so easily as Trey seemed to with her . . .
She'd fallen into believing that friendships weren't to be
trusted either. They were dangerous to get involved in,
because they hurt when they ended . . . and they would
always end.

Now she realized that Trey had simply been protect-
ing himself. And Jake.

And nothing about him had been cold, she realized
now. She had simply sensed the loss of the warmth she'd
felt when she'd been around him. Because he had with-
held that to protect his relationship with Jake. Which she
admired immensely.

"Hey, you two." Jake sailed toward them, then turned
until he glided along the water beside them. "How about
lunch?"

Had Jake noticed a closeness between them, just like
long ago, and this time wanted to stop it short? This time,
had he decided to win Trey no matter what?

No. From everything she'd seen, Jake would give Trey
all the time and space he needed to figure out what he
wanted.

Maybe too much time and space.

———————

After lunch, Jake suggested Danielle take his board and he'd watch while she went solo. She placed the board along the dock and stepped aboard, careful to stay balanced while the board drifted from the wooden planks. She picked up the sail and cautiously shifted it until it caught the wind. It pulled against her arms and she sped up. She shifted it, going faster than she liked, then glided along at a comfortable speed.

She crossed the bay, back and forth, getting a good feel for the board and the sail. A young fellow along her left side sped across the water, then bounced over a cross-wake and fell into the water. Danielle turned to avoid his board and sail as he pulled himself back onto the board.

"Hey, Jeff, good job." Another young man, who looked so much like the man he called Jeff that they must be brothers, stopped beside him. "You're getting better with the speed."

Danielle felt her board picking up speed and quickly tilted the sail and slowed down a little. On shore, Jake waved at her. She turned and glided toward him.

"Dani, you're doing great, but you seem to be afraid to take a chance."

She tipped her head. "What do you mean?"

"It's like you're afraid to get wet. If you want to learn . . . and get really good at windsurfing . . . then you need to push yourself. Take a chance on getting wet."

"But the water's cold."

He jumped into the water and swam toward her board, then grabbed onto it. He flung one arm up and grasped her ankle.

"I think it's time you got wet." He tipped the board as he pulled on her ankle and she plummeted into the water.

She pushed her head above water and sucked in a breath of air, then swam straight for him and lightly whacked him on the side of his head. He chuckled as he wrapped his arm around her and pulled her against his body. His long, hard body.

He pulled her in for a kiss, and as soon as his warm lips met hers, she forgot all about the cold of the water.

He grinned at her. "So now you're wet, you can take some chances. Hop back on the board and push it. Make some mistakes. You'll have more fun in the long run."

She climbed back onto her board and picked up the sail. She caught the wind, and this time she didn't back off when it pulled her past her comfort zone. She rode the wind. Faster and faster. When she found she was getting a little far out, she eased the boom around—too fast, and tumbled into the water. Quickly, she climbed back on the board. As she sped toward shore again, she saw Jake waving at her, a big smile on his face.

She swung her boom around, trying to turn faster than she had before, and tumbled into the water again. She pulled herself up and began again. After a few tries, and several falls, she could turn her board fairly fast and, although a little wobbly, without falling.

"You're doing great, Danielle." Trey pulled in behind her, matching her speed. "You're really improving."

"I took Jake's advice. He told me I should take some chances and not be afraid of falling in."

He nodded. "Good advice."

Thirteen

Trey sipped his green tea, then set the cup on the coffee table. Hickory lay curled up beside him, purring softly. Trey petted him as he flipped through the channels on the television, but nothing interesting caught his eye. Of course, he'd much rather be sitting here with Danielle. She'd left only an hour ago and he missed her already.

The phone rang. He crossed to the computer desk and grabbed the phone from the dock.

"Hi, Trey. It's Suzie. How's it going?"

Suzie was a couple of years younger than he and still lived in Baltimore, where he'd grown up with his family, and where both his younger sisters and his parents still lived. Suzie had her own place, but Tasha, the youngest, was still in high school, so she still lived with his mom and dad.

"Pretty good. Tasha is thinking about which universities she might go to and she's considering Carleton Falls. I suggested we come for a visit to check out the campus . . . and visit with our big brother. So what do you say? Can we stay with you?"

"Yeah, absolutely. When? I'll arrange to take a few days off to spend time with you."

"Well, if it's okay . . . next weekend works out for us. We could come up Friday and stay until the following Friday. Maybe even the weekend."

He walked toward the desk and glanced at the calendar. "I shouldn't have any problem getting the time off, and I'd love to have you both visit."

"Why don't you invite your new girlfriend over while we're there? I'd love to meet her."

"Girlfriend?"

"Danielle, silly. Remember I talked to her on Friday?"

Danielle. Oh, damn. He wouldn't be able to see Danielle for a weekend, possibly two. He did not want to go that long. But he couldn't very well have her stay here with him and Jake. Maybe she could stay at Jake's house. But he couldn't really sneak away to spend time with her while his sisters were here. He wanted to see his sisters, and if he visited her at Jake's, he would spend more time away from his sisters than with them.

"You know, we've never met one of your girlfriends. Rumors are starting about you."

Trey almost dropped the phone. It was just a silly, teasing remark. She didn't mean anything by it . . . but what if she did suspect? What if his family thought he didn't like women? What if they thought he was gay?

He'd worried about it so much during his teenage years when he'd thought he *was* gay. Then when he and Jake had become a couple, he had hidden it from his family. As far as they knew, Jake had simply been his roommate.

He didn't think they'd stop loving him, but he honestly didn't know if they'd be disappointed in him. Even if they accepted it, would things be awkward between them? Would they look at him differently?

"So what do you say?" Suzie asked.

Danielle glanced at the clock. Trey had e-mailed her at work today asking what time she would get home, telling her he wanted to call her to ask about something. It was 5:35 P.M. so he should be calling any minute. She sat down on the couch with the cordless phone on the side table and picked up her book. She'd start cooking dinner after the call.

What did he want to talk to her about? Probably something about plans for the weekend. Maybe he'd gotten tickets to the new play at the local theater and he wanted to check times with her or something.

She stared at the phone, but it did not ring. A knock sounded at her front door. She stood up and walked to the entrance, then peered through the narrow window beside the door.

Trey!

She pulled open the door. "What are you doing here?" she asked.

"I told you I wanted to talk to you, and I thought, Hey, what the heck . . . why not take you to dinner?"

"You came all the way here to take me to dinner?"

He stepped forward and pulled her into his arms, then captured her mouth with his. The feel of his hard, muscular body pressed against the length of hers, his lips caressing hers, his hands cupping her head while he consumed her mouth with passion, sent her heart thundering in her chest.

He smiled at her. "Of course. I missed you. In fact, I started missing you the moment you left my house on Sunday."

His words insinuated their way into her heart and her lips turned up in a broad smile. She felt wanted. And she liked the feeling.

She drew him into the house and pushed the door closed behind him.

"Well, you can't show me how much you missed me if we're out at a restaurant."

"You're not hungry?"

"Oh, I am hungry. For you." She stroked her hand over his growing bulge.

He growled and stroked down her back as he pulled her closer against him, then nuzzled her neck. She unfastened his shirt button, then the next, but he brushed her hands aside and flicked open the buttons on his cuffs, dragged the shirt over his head, and tossed it aside. She tugged her T-shirt over her head and threw it on top of his shirt. A moment later, they'd both shed their jeans in a heap on the floor.

"Oh God, you are gorgeous." Heat simmered in his cinnamon eyes.

Trey gazed at her perfect body. Her lacy black bra was embroidered with red roses across the top of the cups, and the satiny swell of her breasts above made him long to stroke them. Her long, slender legs seemed to go on forever, punctuated by the black thong with roses that matched her bra. She somehow managed to look sweet and pretty yet at the same time totally seductive.

He drew her against his body, enjoying the feel of her satin-soft skin against his. He wrapped his arms around her, pulling her tight to him, and kissed her. Her lips moved sweetly beneath his. His groin tightened and his heart rate accelerated. Her breathing increased and he could tell she was as turned on as he was.

Her hand slid between them and she dipped into his boxers. He groaned at the feel of her hand enveloping his cock.

"Mmm. You really do want me," she said.

He kissed her again, gliding his tongue inside her mouth and swirling it against hers.

"You bet I do."

She unfastened her bra, revealing her round, dusty-rose-tipped breasts. She flung the lacy garment to the side, then pressed against him. Her bead-hard nipples burned into his chest, sending his blood boiling and his cock twitching. He cupped one delectable breast and stroked it, loving the feel of her nipple pressing into his palm.

He leaned down and licked the tight bud, then sucked it into his mouth. She moaned, her fingers raking through his hair as she held him tight to her. He suckled and licked, listening to her increased heartbeat and her sweet little gasps of breath.

"Sweetheart, I want you so badly." He kissed her as he pressed her back until she was against the wall.

He nuzzled the pulse point at the base of her neck, then kissed downward, over the swell of her breasts. He licked her nipple, toying with it on the end of his tongue, then wrapped his lips around it and sucked. She moaned. He switched to the other nipple and sucked mercilessly. She stroked her hands through his hair, then over his shoulders.

He kissed down her lovely flat belly, then across the top of her lacy thong. He smiled up at her, then hooked his fingers under the elastic and pulled. The sight of her curls being revealed as the lace slipped downward made his cock harden more. He continued past her hips, knees, then to her ankles. He wrapped his hand around her heel and lifted her foot, drawing the undies free, then released them from the other foot and tossed them aside. He kissed her calf, nuzzled her knee, then kissed up her thighs. She whimpered in anticipation.

As he closed in on her curls, he shifted to the left, kissing beside them. He stroked over the silky hairs, then slid his finger over the flesh between. Moist and slick. He pressed inside, gliding two fingers into her hot, welcoming opening.

"You are so ready for me."

She simply whimpered for more. With his other hand, he pressed her folds apart and flicked his tongue over her eager clit. She moaned. He licked, then swirled over her as his fingers stroked inside her.

"Oh God, that feels so good," she murmured.

His cock ached to be inside her. He stood up and wrapped his arms around her, then lifted her off the ground. Her legs wrapped around him as he backed her toward the wall and leaned her against it. He pressed the tip of his rock-hard cock against her.

"Oh, Trey." She clung to him, her arms encircling his shoulders.

He pressed forward, easing his cock into her sweet

depths a little at a time. She tightened around him, squeezing him as he glided deeper. Finally, he was fully inside her, pressing her hard to the wall, wondering how she could breathe . . . but she did, and rapidly. He captured her lips again and kissed her with passion as he drew back and thrust into her again. She moaned into his mouth. He dodged his tongue between her lips as he pulled back and plunged into her again . . . and again. His tongue darted forward with each thrust . . . and she murmured her pleasure.

As he thrust, he could feel her tighten . . . her legs around his waist, her vagina around his cock. Her entire being seemed to tighten like a spring. . . . Then she pulled her mouth free and wailed long and loud, her body shuddering with the force of her orgasm.

As her pussy tightened around his blazing hot cock, he felt his release building. He thrust into her, loving the feel of her around him. . . . Then he could feel it . . . close . . . closer.

"Oh, yeah. Sweetheart." He clung to her as she stroked his hair, shooting deep and hard into her. Into the welcoming heat of her body.

As his body relaxed, he held her close, loving the feel of her in his arms. So soft and warm. Her lips trailed along his jaw, then she nibbled his chin. Her legs slid down his hips then to the floor.

"I am so glad you came to see me." She smiled. "That was truly spectacular."

He kissed her, then gazed into her big green eyes.

"I came to ask you if . . . would you be . . . my girl-friend?"

Fourteen

At Danielle's shocked expression, Trey swore under his breath. What kind of an idiot was he to blurt that out? With her in his arms, his cock still embedded in her, he had known. He wanted her to be his woman. And his alone. But right now she was in a relationship with both him and Jake.

For her, was the attraction being with two men? But, no, she wasn't the type to take advantage of people. If she was having sex with him . . . and Jake . . . it was because she felt something for them, even if it wasn't all-out love.

Of course it wasn't love. They had a very unconventional relationship to say the least. He certainly understood those. After all, that's what he'd had with Nikki and Angela back in college.

It was different with Dani, though. He found himself longing for more than just sex with her.

Just what did she feel for him? And for Jake?

He wanted her to be his, but what about Jake? Would Jake be okay with that, or did he want her, too? He'd given no indication.

Damn, this was getting complicated.

But right now, Dani still stared at him in shock.

"I don't mean for real."

At that, her face crinkled in confusion.

"I mean, my sisters are coming to visit me and . . . I was hoping you'd pose as my girlfriend."

Danielle blinked. When he'd asked her to be his girlfriend, her heart had leapt in joy. Then it had crashed down as she saw the conflicting emotions flickering in his eyes. It's like he'd immediately wanted to withdraw his request.

She'd been a fool to actually believe he'd want more from their relationship than what they had. Fun, unconventional, and exciting sex.

And she didn't want him to want more. She wanted him to wind up with Jake. Trey and Jake were meant to be together. She couldn't come between them.

But, of course, she wouldn't. He just wanted her to *pose* as his girlfriend, not *be* his girlfriend.

"Uh . . . sure. I could do that."

"Don't you want to know when?"

"Oh, yes. When?"

"Well, they're coming on Friday and they'll be here all week. If you could come even just for the weekend and stay with me—"

"I can stay the whole week . . . if you want me to."

A lot of her clients were on vacation, so next week was a good time.

He grinned and drew her against him. "I would *love* for you to come for the week." He kissed her, stealing her breath away.

"So why do you want me to pose as your girlfriend?" Danielle asked as she gazed at Trey over the candle on the red-and-white checked tablecloth in the small pizzeria they'd chosen for dinner.

"When Suzie talked to you on the phone last Saturday, she assumed you were my girlfriend, and . . . well, she asked to meet you."

"Okay, but you could have told her that I wasn't."

"My sisters have never met one of my girlfriends."

"Did you think a woman would get the wrong idea, being introduced to your family?"

He glanced at their joined hands. "No. As pathetic as it sounds, I've never really dated a woman long enough to call her a girlfriend."

"What about men?"

His gaze sharpened. "What about them?"

"Have you dated a man long enough to call him a boy-friend? Besides Jake, I mean."

She didn't know if she'd overstepped the bounds of their relationship by asking this question, but after all, he'd just fucked her silly. Surely she was entitled to a personal question or two.

He took a bite of his lasagna and chewed, gazing at her long enough that she thought he wouldn't answer.

"No," he said finally. He sipped his wine, then set the glass down carefully. "I haven't been with a man since Jake. Just women."

"Is it because you haven't been attracted to anyone else?"

He grabbed the crusty loaf of Italian bread and tore a hunk off, his lips a tight straight line. "This is a little off topic."

"I just wonder if maybe you're—"

He jabbed his knife into the butter and slathered it across the white fluffy bread in quick short strokes. "Dani, I don't want to talk about this. We need to figure out our story—how we met, how long we've been dating, et cetera."

"Okay. Well, we met at the university. I already told her that on the phone. We could keep it simple and stay as close to the truth as possible. We met again at Harmony's wedding and started our relationship then."

"But that's only a few weeks. They won't think that's serious."

"I'm the first woman you've introduced to them." She smiled. "They'll believe we're serious."

Danielle pulled up to the university and parked in the lot by the small lake, then walked toward the philosophy building. She'd offered to come to town a day early and help Trey prepare for his sisters' visit, and he'd jumped at the idea. He'd suggested she bring some personal items to leave around the house, but she wasn't quite sure what. She'd never even left a toothbrush at a man's place before. Not even now that she was visiting Trey and Jake every weekend. Maybe he wouldn't mind if she actually left a few spare toiletries at his house so she didn't have to keep carrying them back and forth.

Finally, she'd decided they should take a picture of the two of them, print it up, and put it in a frame. That should be pretty convincing. She arrived early so they could meet up with Jake and have him snap the picture for them. Something in daylight at the university so it didn't look like they'd just taken it.

It was also a great excuse to visit Jake before she went over to Trey's. She didn't know if she'd see him much over the next week, and she missed him.

She strolled along the path across campus to the philosophy building, walked up the stairs to the second floor, then turned right. She stepped into a quieter corridor, leaving the classrooms behind. Offices with professors' names on the doors lined the hallway. She approached the last office. PROFESSOR J. JAMIESON. As she was about to knock on the door, it opened and a young woman in tight jeans and a form-fitting sweater stepped out. She glanced at Danielle, then continued down the hall.

Danielle peered inside. "Professor Jamieson?"

Jake glanced up, then grinned. "Yes, Miss Rayne? What can I do for you?"

With an opening like that, how could she resist? She closed the door behind her and flicked the lock.

"Well, Professor, I haven't been doing very well in your class and I was wondering if there was anything I could do to"—she smiled demurely—"you know . . . improve my marks."

His face shifted to a serious expression. "Like a bonus assignment? I could probably work up something that you could turn in next week."

"I was thinking maybe something I could do right now." She stepped toward him with a sway to her hips.

"Oh?" His eyebrows arched upward. "And exactly what do you have in mind, Miss Rayne?"

She unfastened the top button of her blouse . . . then the next . . . then the next . . . then drew the fabric aside to reveal her lace-covered breasts.

"It depends on what you like." She walked around his

desk and leaned against it, facing him. She dipped her fingers under the lace cups and toyed with her nipples until they jutted forward, then tucked the lace below her breasts, leaving them bare.

She placed one hand on his denim-clad thigh and glided upward, stopping short of the bulge forming in his pants.

"I could do something for you." She stroked over his bulge, then tugged his zipper down and slid her hand inside his pants. His long, hard cock, still covered by the thin cotton of his briefs, pulsed under her fingertips. She slipped her hand inside his briefs and encircled his hot, hard flesh. She knelt in front of him as she freed his erection.

"Oh, Dr. Jamieson. Your cock is enormous."

She leaned down and lapped at the tip like an ice-cream cone, laving over the cockhead, then swirling her tongue under the ridge.

"It's so big, I'm not sure I can even take it in my mouth."

"Of course, you shouldn't be doing that at all, young lady."

She smiled. "But I really want an A."

She licked her lips, then wrapped them around him and made a show of gliding down his crown as if having trouble making it fit. Finally, she held the whole corona in her mouth and glided her tongue around and around.

His fingers forked through her hair and he held her

head gently as she sucked on him, then squeezed him in her mouth. She pushed downward, taking his shaft deeper. So deep she gagged slightly, but relaxed her throat . . . and took him deeper still.

He groaned as she squeezed and sucked, then slipped her hand below to cup his balls and gently massage him with her fingers. He stroked her hair, pushing strands behind her ears. She drew back, then dove down. Back, then dove down again.

She bobbed up and down, stroking his balls all the while. Finally, he groaned and hot liquid filled her throat.

She released his cock, a broad smile on her face.

"So what do you think, Professor Jamieson? Does that deserve an A?"

"I . . . ah . . ."

She didn't want this to end just yet, so she headed off his response.

"Oh, Professor, do you think I've been a bad girl?" She turned around and drew her skirt up, then leaned forward on the desk, revealing her essentially naked behind. "Maybe you should punish me."

"Well, you are pretty naughty, coming in here and doing something like that. You deserve to be punished."

She wiggled her behind back and forth. His hand stroked over her round flesh, and then she felt a sharp sting as he lightly smacked her bottom.

"Ohhh!"

He smacked again, then stroked. Her flesh smarted a little, but it was exhilarating.

"I am such a bad girl, sir. Maybe you should spank me again."

His hand smacked across her burning flesh a couple more times, then his lips pressed against her, easing the sting . . . then stimulating other exciting sensations as he kissed one cheek, then the other.

"Acknowledging your need for punishment will raise your mark to a C." His hands cupped her behind and he stroked round and round.

"And for an A, sir?"

He stood up and she heard the rustle of fabric, then the clunk of his pants, and belt, hitting the floor. His hands slipped around her body and he cupped her naked breasts. They filled his hands as he gently squeezed them within his palms.

"Let's just see if you're worthy of a B right now. Are you willing to do what it takes to get a B?"

"Of course, sir. Whatever you want me to do, sir."

"Actually . . ." His hand stroked down her rib cage and over her belly, then around to unfasten her skirt. He slipped it over her hips and down to her ankles. "*You* won't be doing all that much."

He urged her thighs apart, and she stepped out of the skirt tangled around her ankles, then widened her legs. He stroked down her back, then along the thong as it disappeared between her still stinging cheeks, until he reached the crotch. He drew the fabric aside and dipped his fingers inside.

"My, you are a naughty girl. You are so wet."

And she was. She couldn't believe how turned on she was.

Two of his fingers slipped inside, then he drilled them into her several times.

"Yes, sir. I am so bad. My pussy is so wet."

Her face burned at the words. She never used the word "pussy," but then, right now she was a bad coed who used words she shouldn't.

"Pussy?" He smacked her bottom again. "That isn't a word a nice girl should use."

"I know, sir. I shouldn't say 'pussy.' I shouldn't tell you how wet my pussy is . . . or how much I'd like a nice hard cock to ram into my pussy . . . really hard. . . ."

He smacked her bottom again, then placed the tip of his cock against her.

"Oh, sir. You shouldn't put your cock in my pussy. You shouldn't fuck me. Maybe I should spank *you*."

He thrust forward, fully impaling her in one stroke.

"Oh God, sir. Your big cock feels so good in my wet pussy."

He grabbed her breasts and stroked them roughly, then tugged on her nipples. "You are so bad." He stroked his cheek against hers, then nipped her earlobe.

"Yes, sir. So bad. I want to be fucked by you so bad."

He groaned, then thrust into her again. And again.

His cock stretched her as it drove into her over and over. That and his rough caresses on her breasts sent her heartbeat racing.

Pleasure rose in her with every thrust. He groaned in her ear as he drilled into her.

"Oh, Professor Jamieson. Make me come."

Heat wafted through her. Intense, burning pleasure.

He squeezed her breasts. "I want my bad girl to come right now."

As if by magic, on his command an orgasm exploded within her. She gasped, then expelled a long breath as the pleasure spun through her in a dizzying wave of bliss.

He kept thrusting, then pulled her tight against him as he released inside her.

After a few moments, he loosened his hold on her and drew his spent cock from inside her, then fell back in his chair.

She turned around to face him.

"Okay, so what do I do to get an A?"

He chuckled. "You tell me."

Danielle pulled on his tie to draw him to his feet, then pushed him onto one of his visitor's chairs—one with no armrests—and climbed on his lap. She stroked her fingers over her breasts, watching the heat simmer in his blue eyes. She tucked her hands under each mound, lifting them, then offered him one. He took the rosy bud into his mouth and sucked while she eased his semirigid cock inside her. The feel of his mouth on her nipple sent thrilling sensations spiraling through her. She rotated her hips first one way, then the other, swirling him inside her.

His cock swelled within her. She rocked and swirled around and around, grinding her pelvis into his. Soon his cock was rock hard and standing tall. Still inside her.

"Oh . . ." The first wave of a new orgasm caught her off guard.

He wrapped his hands around her waist and helped her keep her rhythm. She began moving up and down, driving him deeper inside her. The pleasure intensified, until she moaned in pure ecstasy as his cock continued to plunge inside her. Deep and hard.

Just as her pleasure eased off, he erupted inside her.

She wrapped her arms around his neck and held him close, loving the feel of his hard body against her . . . and inside her.

He kissed her ear.

"I definitely think that deserved an A plus."

"So do you think Trey's sisters will like me?" Danielle asked.

"Of course they will." Jake slid his arm around her on the wooden bench as they watched five baby ducklings waddle after their mother as she led them to the small lake. Sunlight glittered through the trees as the leaves rustled in the light breeze.

She wasn't sure about meeting Trey's sisters. It made her nervous. Maybe because she'd never had a sister. Nor a brother. The girls she'd been in the group foster home with hadn't been very close. Usually, they hadn't gotten along and they'd bickered about things.

Would Trey's sisters judge her as unfit for their brother? It shouldn't matter to her—she wasn't in a real romance with Trey—but it was important to him.

"I'm not sure how to act around them."

"Just be yourself . . . and act like you're head over heels for Trey."

"You don't mind? You're not jealous?"

"Well, maybe a little."

The serious look in his eyes made her wonder. She had meant was he jealous that she would be monopolizing Trey's time, and affection, but she could almost believe he was jealous of Trey being with her.

Of course, that was just wishful thinking. Jake might like having sex with her and Trey, but it was Trey he loved.

"I asked Trey about his interest in men and he said he hasn't been with a man since he was with you. When I tried to push him on it, he changed the subject. That, and the fact he wants his sisters to believe he has a girlfriend when he's never found a woman he's interested in enough for a long-term relationship, tell me that he is in a state of denial."

Jake stretched his arms along the back of the bench. "I agree."

"Do you really think his family will think less of him if they find out he likes men?"

Jake shrugged. "I don't think so, but it's hard to say. Since Trey is very close to his family and it would devastate him if this caused a barrier between them, I understand his caution."

"I guess so." She'd never had a family, but she could see that if she had, she would never want to do anything to alienate them. Still, denying who you are to meet someone else's criteria . . . especially when you're not even sure of those criteria . . . seemed a little extreme.

"There's Trey now."

She glanced in the direction of Jake's gaze and saw Trey ambling along the walkway toward them. She and Jake stood up and walked toward him. Trey took her in his arms and kissed her, then smiled.

"Hey, girlfriend. Let's go have our picture taken."

"They're here."

Danielle glanced toward Trey, who stood at the window peering out.

He seemed so nervous. She couldn't help feeling he didn't think his sisters would like her. She picked up the pewter frame that contained the photo they'd printed off less than an hour ago. She and Trey looked like a perfect couple. He'd grabbed a handful of her long red waves and had pulled her in for a kiss, then they'd glanced toward the camera, their cheeks pressed together, Trey with a silly grin on his face, and her . . . well, she almost beamed.

Jake had taken about a hundred pictures, trying to get the ideal candid shot. He'd done a good job. She and Trey looked happy together. Like a perfect match.

She set the picture on the side table again. Trey walked toward the door, Hickory following on his heels. As soon as Trey opened the door, Hickory raced outdoors.

Danielle stood up and brushed at her pants, smoothing the fabric, then stepped toward the door. A petite brunette walked up the stone path leading to the front door, a taller, slim teenager following behind her.

"Trey!" The older sister, Suzie, launched herself at Trey and he threw his arms around her, then gave her a big kiss.

The younger sister—Trey had said her name was Tasha—stood demurely behind Suzie. When Trey released Suzie he smiled broadly at his youngest sister.

"Tasha. You've grown so much." He held open his arms and she stepped into them.

She might have gone into the hug hesitantly, but

Danielle could see her arms tighten around her older brother. Trey kissed her, then picked up their bags and carried them down the hall to their bedrooms . . . leaving Danielle staring at the two of them.

"You must be Danielle," Suzie said, smiling warmly.

Fifteen

Danielle held out her palm to shake hands but Suzie laughed and threw her arms around Danielle, giving her a warm hug. When she released Danielle, who had stiffened at the unexpected contact, Tasha stepped forward and hugged Danielle, too. Her slim arms encircled Danielle's body and she gave a quick squeeze, then stepped back.

"Great, you three have managed the introductions," Trey said as he returned to the room. "Dinner will be ready in about twenty minutes. Do you want something to drink?"

Trey led them into the kitchen, where his sisters sat on the tall stools at the counter eating area. Danielle opened the fridge and took out the pitchers of lemonade and iced tea that she'd prepared earlier and placed them on the counter. Trey placed four glasses on the counter beside the frosty pitchers.

"We're having lasagna for dinner, since I know how much you love it, Tasha," Trey said.

"With garlic bread and Caesar salad?" she asked as she poured herself some lemonade.

"Of course." Trey sipped his iced tea. "How was the drive?"

"Great," Suzie answered. "Good weather all the way here." She glanced at Danielle. "So, Danielle, what do you do?"

"Me? Oh, I'm self-employed. I develop Web sites for small businesses."

"That's sounds like fun. Do you work from home?"

"Mostly, though I do spend some time with my clients determining their needs. What about you?"

Trey placed a tray on the counter with a selection of cheese and crackers and a few red grapes as garnish, then went to the sink, where he began washing lettuce for the salad. Tasha popped a grape into her mouth, and Danielle took a slice of cheddar and placed it atop a stone-ground whole wheat cracker.

"I'm a guidance counselor at a high school."

"At the same high school Tasha goes to?" Danielle asked.

"Oh God, no," Tasha said in such an animated voice, especially given her quiet demeanor so far, it caught Danielle off guard. "That would be awful. My sister working at the school I go to!"

Danielle would have thought it would be great, but she wasn't really an expert on sister relationships. Didn't Tasha and her sister get along?

"Don't mind her. No teenager wants her big sister anywhere near her friends . . . or her social circle."

"So, little Tasha is going to university next year," Trey said as he sat down on the stool beside his youngest sister.

Tasha didn't look all that little. She was tall and slim with a well-proportioned figure, long straight dark hair, and the same warm brown eyes with gold specks that Trey had. Whether Trey saw it or not, she was definitely a young woman.

They chatted for a while, then Trey served dinner. They made plans to visit the university the next day, mostly for just a look-see, since it was a Saturday. They'd do a full tour on Monday.

After cleaning up the dishes, they all watched a movie in the living room before calling it a night.

Danielle followed Trey into the bedroom and closed the door behind her, feeling odd going in there with him while his sisters were in the house.

"So, what do you think of Suzie and Tasha?"

"They're beautiful—and so nice."

He stroked her cheek. "Then why do you look per-plexed?"

"No, it's just that . . . I found it weird . . ."

"What's weird?"

"They hugged me. When they first got here. But they don't even know me."

He pulled her into his arms and hugged her. She leaned against his familiar warm chest.

"Danielle, you're my girlfriend. That means you're part of the family."

Part of the family. As simple as that. She would love to be part of his family. To have many more nights like the one they'd just had. To feel like she belonged.

After changing into her nightgown, she climbed into bed beside Trey. As nice as the evening had been, as she lay there, it felt like something was missing. It took her only a moment to realize that . . . it felt strange lying in bed beside Trey without Jake.

In the morning, Danielle blinked open her eyes as bright summer sunshine washed across her face.

"Time to get up," Trey said as he stood by the window fastening the last few buttons on his shirt.

She rolled onto her back, away from the glare, and tucked her hands behind her head.

He strolled to the bed and prowled to her side.

"Looking sexy to entice me back to bed won't work." He rolled over her, planting a hand on each side of her shoulders, and leaned down to kiss her, then nuzzled her neck. "Well, maybe it *will* work."

Delicious tingles danced through her body and she longed to rip open her nightgown and pull him into her depths. Instead, she flattened her hands against his chest . . . his hard sculpted muscular chest . . . and pressed him away, still very conscious of the fact that his sisters were nearby.

"No, we really do need to get up," she said.

Trey kissed her again, then rolled away. "Okay, but if you change your mind . . ."

"I know." She grinned. "You're ready and willing."

She disappeared into the bathroom, the gentle caress of his lips still haunting her. She showered, pulled on a pair of jeans and a turquoise T-shirt, and headed toward the kitchen.

"Morning, Danielle." Tasha glanced up from the magazine she was reading while sitting on the couch in the sunny living room. Hickory lay by the window in a patch of sunlight on the carpet.

"Good morning, Tasha. Did you sleep well?"

"Uh-huh. Trey and Suzie are in the kitchen making breakfast."

Danielle nodded and pushed through the door.

"Hey, Dani. Want a coffee?" At her nod, Trey poured some coffee into one of the tall red stoneware mugs he knew she liked and handed it to her.

"May I help with something?"

"No, you just enjoy your coffee," said Suzie. "Trey and I have this under control."

"But—"

"Really. Trey and I work well together."

Danielle poured a little cream in her coffee and a teaspoon of sugar, then sat at the counter and watched them. They did work well together, Trey turning the sizzling bacon, then pulling it out with tongs and placing it on a stack of paper towels to drain, while Suzie poured the beaten eggs into a frying pan, then glided a wooden spoon back and forth in the pan. The toaster popped up and Trey tossed the toast onto a plate, put a couple more slices of bread into the toaster, then buttered the fresh toast.

She sipped her coffee while she watched them move around the kitchen handling the various tasks like a real team. It probably seemed like the simplest, most ordinary day in the world to Trey and his sisters, but to Danielle, the simple pleasure of a morning breakfast with family seemed like the best thing in the entire world.

Finally, breakfast was ready, and they all sat down at the dining room table, which Tasha had set, to enjoy the hot breakfast together. The kidding and camaraderie around the table made Danielle realize just how much she'd missed by never being a part of a close group of siblings.

As they finished, Suzie said, "Is your friend Jake joining us for dinner tonight?"

"I didn't ask him, so no. It's just us tonight."

Danielle noticed a hint of disappointment in Suzie's

eyes, then it quickly dissappeared. "But we could invite him," Danielle said.

"Really?" Suzie perked up. "I mean, I haven't seen him in years and I just thought, well, it might be nice to catch up."

"Sure, I'll call him and invite him along," Trey said with a shrug.

Suzie turned her gaze to her eggs, but Danielle noticed the twinkle in her eyes. *Uh-oh.* Maybe this wasn't such a good idea. Suzie had no idea how . . . complicated . . . things were between the three of them, and she knew Trey would die if she found out.

In the short time she'd known Suzie, Danielle had begun to feel a strong attachment to her, and she didn't like the idea of her being disappointed.

Jake stepped into the busy restaurant and noticed Danielle and Trey sitting side by side, looking very cozy, with Suzie across from them. Suzie smiled at him brightly.

"Hello everyone." He sat down beside Suzie as they all greeted him.

"You remember my sister Suzie," Trey said.

"Of course."

He'd met Suzie on a couple of occasions over the years, but they'd never spent more than a few minutes together. She wore a stylish black dress with a plunging neckline, her dark hair swept into an elegant up-do. She certainly looked a lot different than she had when Jake and Trey were in college. Back then she'd had braces and glasses and been painfully shy, her head always buried in a book.

"And where's Tasha?" Jake asked.

"She has friends in town," Suzie said.

"Ah." That was answer enough. Any teenager would rather hang out with friends rather than a bunch of *old* people like them.

It was strange sitting across from Danielle, as she and Trey sat close together, acting like lovers—exclusive lovers—while he just watched. He longed to slide in beside Danielle and stroke her long, silky thigh, to kiss her warm, full lips . . . but tonight, she was Trey's girlfriend.

"Jake, I was surprised to hear that you're still single," Suzie said as she eyed the menu. "There must be a lot of women in your life, a handsome guy like you."

As she smiled warmly at him, then tucked some loose strands of glossy dark hair behind her ear, he got the distinct impression that shy little Suzie was flirting with him—and quite brazenly, too. Which made things damn awkward. He'd be the first to admit that his sex life was unconventional, if not downright wild, but he sure as hell wasn't going to make a move on Trey's little sister. Just the idea was creepy as hell.

"Actually I don't date a lot of women." He ever so

slightly emphasized the word "women" and winked at Trey and Danielle.

Suzie didn't seem to notice, but Trey's gaze darted to the menu and he cleared his throat.

"I have a lot going on in my life right now," Jake continued. "Not much time to date."

Throughout dinner, Suzie showed great interest in Jake's work. Trey and Danielle kept involved in the conversation, too, but Danielle seemed a little distracted. Jake wondered if Trey was stroking her leg, or if she was stroking Trey. Jake longed to feel her hand graze his leg, then stroke over his rising bulge. . . . He was getting hot at the thought of being with her again. Wishing he could be with her right now.

When she rose to go to the ladies' room, he wanted to excuse himself, too, and drag her into the men's room for some dirty exciting sex in a stall. But Suzie went with her.

An awkward silence between Jake and Trey followed, which he had never experienced with Trey, and Jake was glad when Danielle and Suzie returned. The awkwardness between Trey and himself was weird, but he realized it was a natural result of the fact that Danielle's acting as Trey's girlfriend had changed the balance of the relationship among the three of them. Right now, Jake was an outsider. He wasn't allowed to touch Danielle, or hold her.

To kiss her. He had to treat her like his friend's girlfriend. The problem was, it felt all too real. Jake felt like a fifth wheel, and he didn't like it.

Man, he wished this week were over so things could get back to normal. So he could ravage Danielle within an inch of her life.

Danielle waited beside Suzie and Jake as Trey unlocked the car and opened the passenger door for her.

"Actually, I was going to ask Danielle if she could ride in my car to the club," Jake said.

"I could ride with you," Suzie suggested.

"Well, I wanted to get Danielle's advice about something."

"That's a great idea," said Danielle, stepping in. "I'd love to give you some advice."

Suzie looked disappointed, but she got into Trey's car.

"I'm parked around here," Jake said.

Danielle followed him along the parking lot, then around the building. As soon as they turned the corner and were out of sight of Trey's car, he dragged her into his arms and captured her lips. His mouth assaulted hers with passion, and when he finally released her, she was breathless.

"God, I've missed you."

She smiled at him. "You saw me only yesterday."

"I guess, but . . . now it feels like you really are Trey's girlfriend and I'll never be with you again."

Forbidden Heat

She wrapped her arms around his neck and pressed her body close. "It's just pretend, remember?"

"I just hope you two do."

They walked to his gorgeous red Mustang and he opened the door for her. He settled into the driver's seat beside her, then took her into his arms for another passionate kiss. His hands began to rove over her body. When he lightly caressed her breasts, her nipples blossomed in need. She stroked her hand down his hard chest, over his stomach. As she grazed over his growing bulge, she felt heat growing in her belly and rising through her body.

She wanted to tug out his big cock and swallow it down right now, then climb on top of him and glide it inside her.

A car engine started behind them, and reluctantly, she drew away from him.

"We really should be going. They'll be waiting for us."

Trey watched Jake and Danielle walk to the table where he was sitting with Suzie waiting for them. They had taken a long time to get here and Jake's hand was resting on Danielle's lower back as they walked together. Had they stopped for a quick intimate encounter on the way? Jealousy boiled up in him, but he realized they hadn't taken that long getting here.

What the hell was wrong with him? Why did the thought of Jake spending time with Danielle . . . being *intimate* with Danielle . . . drive him crazy? After all, they'd been sharing the woman for weeks now.

Danielle sat down beside him and he breathed in the subtle herbal fragrance of her hair. He slid his arm around her and drew her close.

"Hi, sweetheart." He kissed her, loving the feel of her soft full lips under his.

When they drew apart, he caught Suzie smiling at them. Jake's expression, on the other hand, was unreadable.

"Suzie, would you like to dance?" Jake asked.

"I'd love to."

Jake led Suzie to the dance floor. When he drew Suzie close to his body, his arm around her waist, a brotherly protectiveness rose in Trey. He was extremely conscious of Jake's hand on his little sister's lower back . . . of the way her body pressed against his . . . of the intimacy when he leaned in and murmured in her ear. Trey gritted his teeth. Maybe he should just—

"I think our role-playing is leaving Jake feeling a little left out."

"Did you two do something about that on the way over here?" he asked a little too harshly.

She sent him a sharp questioning gaze. "No. Not really."

But something about her tone made him think something had happened between them.

"You're not really jealous of Jake and me, are you? Remember, I'm just pretending to be your girlfriend."

Trey's chest tightened. She was just *pretending* to be his girlfriend. Although he knew it was true, he now began to question everything. Did she have any real feelings for him? Had it just been about an exciting illicit sexual relationship with two men all along? He'd started having feelings for this woman . . . and more, he'd begun to believe she had feelings for him, too.

And what about her feelings for Jake? Would this whole relationship end up in a competition to win the girl. A competition that would end in the destruction of a friendship— more than a friendship—that had endured for almost sixteen years?

Danielle stepped out of the car in the parking lot by the campus center on Monday morning. The sun was shining but there were a few gray clouds on the horizon. She happily followed Trey and his sisters on a tour of campus, remembering her own time at Carleton Falls University. Tasha would have a great time here. She could spread her wings with confidence, knowing her older brother was close by if she needed support.

After an hour of walking around campus, they went to the campus center and stopped in the little café. After picking up their beverages at the counter, they sat down and relaxed for a few minutes.

"It's eleven now," Trey said, looking at his watch. He turned to Tasha. "We have a meeting with Dr. Gemina at noon. You can ask her about the different programs you might like to apply to."

"It was great she agreed to spend time with Tasha," Suzie said.

Trey smiled. "One of the perks of working at the university. Making great contacts to help your kid sister sort out her future."

Tasha smiled, then took the last sip of her strawberry frappuccino. "I'd like to head to the bookstore now."

Trey stood up, his coffee in hand. Danielle finished her tea as they walked past the other tables, and dropped her empty cup in the garbage near the door as they left the café.

"I'd like to buy another sweatshirt," Suzie said. "The one I got last time is really comfortable, but it's wearing out."

"That's here in the campus center store," Danielle told her. "Do you want to stop there first?"

"No, you all go ahead to the bookstore. I'll meet you over there later. I'd like to browse for a bit."

"Do you want me to show you where it is?" Danielle asked.

"No, I remember. I've been here a bunch of times. Really, I just want to poke around at my own speed."

"Okay, Suzie. See you later," Trey said.

A knock sounded at Jake's office door. He didn't have any appointments this morning. It was probably a student wanting to ask about marks or maybe help understanding the latest essay assignment.

"Come in."

The door opened and Suzie, Trey's sister, popped her head in the door.

"Hi, there," she said.

"Hi. Come on in. What are you doing here?"

Suzie stepped into the office and closed the door behind her. She carried a couple of blue plastic bags he recognized from the campus stores.

"Trey thought it would be a good idea to show Tasha around campus today. Tasha is meeting with a Dr. Gemina at noon."

She sat down in the guest chair facing his desk and placed the bags at her feet.

Jake nodded. "Good idea. She'll be able to help Tasha figure out the best program for her and advise her on what courses to take. She can also suggest scholarships she might be eligible for."

"So . . ." She smiled, looking slightly nervous. "I wanted to stop by and tell you I had a good time last night."

Uh-oh. "Yes, it was fun. The four of us get along well together."

"Sure . . . but I mean specifically . . . I enjoyed being with you." She perched on the edge of the chair. "I felt that there was . . . a bit of a spark between us." She glanced down at her hands, which were clasped in her lap, then back to him. "I don't mean to be forward but . . . I wondered if you might like to get together for dinner one day this week . . . without Trey and Danielle, or Tasha. Just to see if there might be something worth pursuing."

He sighed and stepped out from behind his desk, then perched on the edge, facing her.

"Suzie, I really like you. . . ."

She smiled. "Good."

"But . . . Well, I'm seeing someone."

She stood up and stepped toward him. "And this someone . . . is it serious?"

"Well, uh . . ."

Damn, if she only knew the truth. It would send her running at lightning speed.

She stepped a little too close and her hand brushed across his cheek. "It sounds like the jury's still out on that. So maybe there is a chance for me." She stared at him with her dark brown eyes. "You know, ever since I first met you, I've had kind of a crush on you. I've always wanted to explore the possibilities, but . . . there's never been a chance. I just thought that . . ."

As she stared at him with wide eyes, his gut clenched at having to turn her down. Here she was putting her feelings on the line and . . . he hated having to do this.

"Suzie, you're a very attractive woman and—"

Before he could finish his sentence, she leaned in and kissed him. Her soft lips caught him by surprise, and he tried to jerk back only to realize that her arms were en-circled around his neck, holding him immobile.

He stood up, which only served to bring their bodies tighter together. *Nooo!* This couldn't be happening. This was Trey's sister.

"What the hell is going on here?"

Suzie pulled back and stared around at a very angry-looking Trey standing at the door, Danielle peering in from behind him.

Sixteen

Shock pummeled Danielle at the sight of Jake kissing Suzie. "Oh, Jake, how could you? She's Trey's sister."

Suzie stepped back from Jake and turned toward Trey and Danielle. "If Jake and I want to—"

Trey's fists clenched at his sides. "Suzie, don't. You don't know what you're getting in the middle of here."

She straightened her back. "So maybe you should tell me."

"It's not up to me." He glared at Jake. "And it's not the time. Tasha has an appointment in ten minutes and I thought you wanted to be a part of that."

Suzie sighed. "Yes, of course." She turned to Jake. "We can talk later?"

Jake nodded, knowing he'd have to set her straight.

She walked to the door.

"Tasha's going to meet us there, but we'd better hurry." Trey glanced around at Danielle, who still stood at the door. "Danielle, are you coming?"

"No, you go ahead. You don't need me in the meeting. I was just going to shop around the bookstore a little more anyway."

Trey glanced at her, then at Jake, and nodded his head.

Once they'd disappeared down the hall, she stepped into Jake's office and closed the door.

"Danielle, it wasn't what it looked like."

"That's a little clichéd, isn't it?" She kept her voice light, despite the sick feeling in the depths of her stomach.

"Okay, sure, Suzie was kissing me . . . but I wasn't kissing her back. She came here to tell me she thought there might be something between us. I told her there was someone else."

"And so she decided to jump your bones?"

"No, she's not like that. She asked if my relationship was serious and . . . I can't believe we're even having this conversation. Do you honestly think that with everything going on with you and Trey and me, I'd be sleazy enough to pull Trey's kid sister into the mix? What do you take me for?"

"You're right," Danielle said. "I'm sorry. I saw you two together and . . . it freaked me out that you were ruining your chances with Trey."

"Who are we kidding, Danielle? Wanting to get Trey and me back together again is more your idea than mine."

"But . . . I thought . . ."

He stepped toward her and gently grasped her shoulders. "It's driving me crazy seeing you and Trey as a couple . . . feeling totally outside the relationship." He captured her lips in an intense kiss, then gazed at her with blazing navy blue eyes. "Damn it. What are we doing here, Danielle? You and I . . . and Trey? Where can it lead?" He drew her closer. "I want *you*."

Her heart quivered, both with delight and fear at how this whole thing was flying out of control . . . and might leave all three of them an emotional mess.

"What about Trey?" she asked for a second time.

"Of course I have feelings for Trey, but . . . don't you think if it was going to work out it would have by now? I think I'd be kidding myself to believe that we can pick it up again, and even if we did . . . there was always something missing between us."

Staring into his intense blue eyes, she saw the vulnerability there. He stroked her hair behind her ear with a gentle brush of his fingers.

"But with you . . ." His hesitation left words unsaid. Words she wanted to hear him say.

Finally, he pulled her tight to his chest, his strong arms firm around her.

"God, I want you so much."

Jake wanted to tell her he was falling in love with her . . .
but he couldn't do that. Not now. Not with things so
messed up. But he did show her. He leaned in and kissed her,
his mouth moving on hers with all the pent-up passion
and desire pulsing through him.

She melted against him, her soft breasts crushed against
his chest.

"I want you so badly," he said as he held her tight
against him, stroking her hair. And he didn't mean physically, though his body was thrumming with painful need,
his erection pushing tight against his confining jeans.

"Jake, I . . ." She gazed up at him with her wide emerald eyes. "I want you, too."

He cupped her cheeks and kissed her. He could feel
her hands moving along her blouse, and when he released
her lips, he saw that she'd unfastened the buttons.

Opening to him. Inviting him.

Her sexy pink lace bra accentuated her lovely round
breasts. He stroked over one and she smiled, then lifted her
lips to his. He lifted her onto the desk and she drew her full
skirt upward, revealing her pink lace panties.

He stroked up her silken thighs, then stepped between
them. She ran her hand over his pulsing erection, then released his zipper and reached inside. He almost groaned at
the feel of her delicate hand wrapping around his twitching
near-to-bursting cock.

He wanted to ravage her breasts, to lean down and kiss her pussy until she reached the ultimate orgasm . . . but right now, he needed to be inside her.

Maintaining riveting eye contact, he pressed closer to her. She drew out his cock and pressed it against her pussy, pushing the crotch of her panties aside. He eased forward, slowly pressing himself into her. Her moist heat swallowed his cockhead. He pushed deeper, her hot depths swallowing him slowly, bit by bit.

It was like coming home. Warm. Welcoming.

Loving.

Her body embraced him as he eased inside her.

Once he was fully immersed, he continued to stare into her eyes. He saw a need there . . . as great as his own.

He kissed her, their lips bonding in intense passion. His tongue dipped inside her, diving deep. She answered with a swirl of her tongue.

His cock twitched and she murmured in pleasure. He pressed his hand to her lower back and pulled her tighter to him, pushing deeper still.

"Ohhh . . ." Her eyes darkened and she actually looked close. . . . Sure he was inside her, but he'd hardly done anything. Except kiss her.

She opened her legs wider and wrapped them around him, then arched against him.

His cock pushed impossibly deep into her wonderful heat. He groaned at the intensely erotic sensation.

She clung to his shoulders tightly, as though hovering on the edge, her gaze still locked on his.

He drew back, then glided forward. She tightened around him and arched forward again. Her breathing grew labored. He drew back again, and thrust forward.

"Ohh . . ." She gasped.

As he moved inside her, she moaned. Her eyelids dropped closed briefly—then, as he pulled back again, and dove deep . . . she lost it. Her eyelids fell closed and she moaned with abandon. He thrust and thrust again, watching her lovely face contort in sheer pleasure. His own pleasure built and his body tightened. He captured her lips and kissed her with intense passion. Then . . . he erupted into her in a mind-shattering orgasm.

By two o'clock, Danielle had finished her shopping and sat on a bench outside the bookstore waiting for Trey and his sisters.

"Hi, Danielle." Suzie walked up and sat beside her. "Trey and Tasha will be along in a minute. Listen, I'm sorry about the kerfuffle earlier in Jake's office. I didn't mean to embarrass you or anything."

"It's okay."

"Trey's a bit overprotective and—oh, here they come."

Danielle glanced up to see Tasha and Trey talking together as they walked along the tree-lined path across campus. She and Suzie stood up and joined them as they continued to the car. They made the short drive home in silence.

After dinner, Tasha went out to see her friends again. She'd asked to sleep over a couple of days and Suzie had agreed. Danielle made dinner, so Suzie and Trey insisted on doing the dishes. As Danielle sat in the living room reading, she could hear their conversation in the kitchen.

"I would think you'd be happy about me going out with one of your best friends. Isn't that better than me going out with someone you don't know anything about?"

Dishes clanked together as she dropped them into the water-filled sink with a little too much exuberance.

"He told you he's going out with someone."

"Sure, but he didn't seem too confident about it."

More dishes clanked.

"Look, Trey, I've been interested in Jake for a long time. He's a great guy—you've said that yourself. He's intelligent and interesting and sensitive . . . and on top of that, he's exceptionally good-looking. What more could a girl want?"

What more indeed.

Cutlery clinked on the countertop.

"Suzie, I understand your point, but . . . you just don't understand the whole situation."

"Then enlighten me."

There was a long pause.

"The situation with Jake and this woman is . . . a bit confusing . . . but I know he really cares about her."

Danielle sucked in a breath at the raw emotions welling up in her. If Trey really believed that, then . . . what did he think of this whole situation?

"Confusing how? I don't understand."

"I can't tell you how. It's . . . personal stuff, but . . . Look, Suzie, the woman Jake is dating is . . . a friend of mine. If he throws her over for you . . . I don't want to see her hurt."

Silence hung in the air. Danielle stared at her book, but couldn't concentrate on the words. Trey was being protective of her, and that touched her heart.

"You really like this woman?" Suzie asked.

"Yes."

"More than me?"

Trey chuckled. "You know I don't like *anyone* more than you, Suzie-Q."

Suzie laughed, and from the muffled sound, Danielle bet they were hugging right about now.

"Okay, Trey. I'll back off. But if he breaks up with this woman, I want you to phone me right away . . . and set us up!"

"I'll call you, but you set up your own dates!"

"Deal!"

The next day, Danielle, Trey, and Suzie spent the hot sunny afternoon lying around the pool, with an occasional dip in the water to cool off, then enjoyed barbecued burgers and salad for dinner. Danielle enjoyed chatting with Suzie and Trey about the latest TV shows, movies, books, and current events. Suzie showed a great interest in how people felt about things. Their likes and dislikes. Their hopes and dreams. Not that Danielle revealed much about herself, but Suzie's intense interest made her feel like the woman actually cared. It made her feel even more intensely how she'd love to have a sister.

Finally, once the sun set and the mosquitoes started biting, they gathered up their dishes and moved into the house. After they'd done the dishes, Trey went out back to put the pool cover on to keep the heat in overnight. Danielle and Suzie settled on the couch with a glass of wine.

"Danielle, I hope you don't mind my asking, but how did you wind up in the foster care system?"

Danielle's stomach clenched but she just shrugged. "My mother gave me up."

Suzie sipped her wine. "Have you ever wondered what she was like?"

"No. I know exactly what she was like." She kept her voice even, despite the turmoil thoughts of her mother elicited.

"You weren't a baby when she gave you up?"

"No. I know a lot of women—especially teenagers—give up their babies when they have an unexpected pregnancy, but that's not what happened with me." A lump formed in her throat. "Those kids are lucky because . . . their mothers cared what happened to them . . . or at least gave some thought to it." She picked up her glass and took a sip. "In my case, my mother just . . . didn't care."

"Honey, that's probably not true."

"Oh, it's true." She stared at her wine as she swirled it in the glass, not willing to allow Suzie to see the anger and hurt in her eyes. "One night when I was four years old, my mother just got sick of my crying and . . . shoved me outside and locked the door."

Danielle remembered the absolute terror she'd felt standing outside the house . . . all alone. She had banged on the door and cried, pleading with her mother to let her back in, but the door had remained closed. Later, when she was old enough to understand these things, she'd discovered that her mother was an alcoholic, and if she hadn't been totally plastered, she might have realized what a bad idea it had been to leave her young daughter outside where people could hear her screaming.

Danielle didn't know how long she'd been out there, alone and crying. It had felt like forever.

Suzie shook her head in disbelief, staring at Danielle to assure herself this wasn't some kind of strange joke.

"Oh, Danielle, I'm so sorry." Suzie moved closer.

Knowing Suzie probably wanted to hug her, Danielle stood up and paced the room.

Suzie watched her. "How could she do such a thing?"

"Later, I heard that she'd been pretty drunk that night."

"But that doesn't explain how a mother could treat her child that way." Suzie shook her head. "That was . . . inhuman."

Danielle found herself blinking back tears. She'd lived with this a long time, thought that she was over it . . . or at least immune to the emotional turmoil remembering the event used to cause her. But clearly that wasn't true.

"What happened?" Suzie asked. "Did she finally let you back in?"

Danielle shook her head. "After a while, a neighbor heard me. She came to see if I was okay."

Danielle had backed away, screaming, when the woman had tried to approach her. The poor woman had been frantic to help this scared little girl. She kept saying she just wanted to help, but Danielle had been too frantic . . . too frightened.

"I guess she called someone. I don't really remember." She did remember that the woman had stood about twenty yards away, keeping an eye on her. "Not long after that, the police showed up."

That had terrified her even more. She'd thought they'd

come to arrest her and that they'd throw her into a dark jail cell.

"I don't really remember much after that, except . . . when I finally saw my mother again . . . years later . . ." Danielle's fists clenched by her sides. "She told me she was glad they took me away. I'd always been a pain in the ass to her and she was glad to be rid of me."

"She actually said that?" Suzie asked, her eyes gleaming.

Danielle simply nodded, wondering why in hell she had revealed that.

Suzie stepped toward her and gathered Danielle in her arms.

"I can't believe a mother would do that to a small child. That she would do that to *you*."

Danielle stood stiffly in Suzie's warm embrace. A part of her wanted to relax into the comforting warmth the woman offered her . . . but she couldn't. Remembering her mother brought it all back. The reality was that she was alone in this life . . . and she had to remember that. It wasn't safe to let anyone get close. She couldn't let herself rely on anyone.

"I wish I had been there." Suzie stroked Danielle's back. "I wish I could have held you when you were that little child and told you how special you are."

At those words, tears prickled at Danielle's eyes again.

How different would her life have been if she'd had someone who'd really cared about her? If she'd had someone who would have held her when she'd cried? Who would have really cared when she'd been hurting?

Who would have loved her.

But she hadn't, and there was no point crying over what she couldn't change. She blinked back the tears.

"What's going on?"

Seventeen

At Trey's voice behind her, Danielle drew herself from Suzie's arms. She carefully turned away from Trey so he couldn't see her expression nor the single tear that had escaped despite her resolve.

"Nothing." She stroked her hair behind her ear, dashing away the tear in the process. "I'm going to head to bed now." She strode to the hallway and escaped toward the bedroom.

"Trey." Suzie's voice stopped Trey as he started to follow Danielle.

Danielle slipped into the room and closed the door behind her.

She sat down on the bed and fought back the overwhelming emotions flooding through her at the unwelcome memories. Damn it, she'd thought she'd put all these feelings behind her.

A few moments later, a light tap sounded at the door.

"Danielle, it's Trey. May I come in?"

Damn it. Why couldn't he leave her alone?

"Danielle?"

She cleared her throat, knowing she'd have to answer him.

"Yes." Thankfully, the word came out clearly . . . not a croak as she'd feared.

The door opened and Trey stepped inside, his expression one of concern. He closed the door and approached the bed.

"Suzie told me about your conversation." He sat beside her, concern simmering in his warm brown eyes. "I knew you were in foster care but . . ." He rested his hand on her arm and she fought her instinctive reaction to pull it away. "I had no idea how your mother had . . ." He hesitated, watching her carefully, his expression sympathetic. "How difficult it was for you."

She simply nodded in acknowledgment.

"I should have asked. I wish I had." His lips pursed. "I just didn't want to pry."

"It's okay." Her voice came out hoarse.

"Not that I'm saying Suzie was prying," he went on. "She just naturally asks questions. Because she cares."

Danielle nodded again.

He curled his fingers around her hand. "Are you okay?"

She didn't utter a word, needing all her attention to keep it together.

When she didn't answer, he squeezed her hand, then kissed it. "Danielle? I wish you'd say something."

She sucked in a deep breath, ready to assure him that everything was just fine.

"I'm—"

Her voice cracked, and Trey's heart crumbled. Her eyes were awash with unshed tears and she looked so very . . . vulnerable.

"Oh, sweetheart." He drew her into his arms and held her close.

She sat stiff in his embrace, clearly fighting the overwhelming pain showing in her tortured eyes. Gently, he drew her head against his shoulder, cradling it there with one hand while he held her close with the other.

The thought of her as a small child . . . thrown out into the night . . . terrified and frightened . . . gnawed at him. How could any mother do that to her own child? No wonder Danielle never allowed herself to get close to anyone. To depend on anyone. The one person whom she should have been able to depend on without question . . . who should have loved her unconditionally . . . had betrayed her completely.

"You should never have been treated that way."

At his words, she collapsed against him. Her body shook in sobs and he felt dampness against his shirt. She was shedding the tears she'd been trying so hard to hold back.

He stroked her back, pressing his lips to her soft hair and kissing her gently. A protective instinct flared through him, so strong it nearly bowled him over . . . followed by the realization of just how much he loved this woman.

And if the time was ever right to tell her, it was now. A part of him wanted to hold back, at least until he'd had a chance to talk to Jake—Jake was a part of this relationship, too—but Danielle needed to know she was loved, and right now, that was more important than anything else.

"Danielle, I understand why you've always kept to yourself. Why you've shied away from love. Because you've always believed you were alone. But . . ." He tucked his finger under her chin and tipped her face upward. Rivulets of tears streaked her cheeks. "If I have my way"—his voice lowered to a murmur and he smiled tenderly—"you'll never be alone again."

Her gleaming eyes gazed at him without comprehension.

"Because . . . I'm crazy in love with you."

"You're . . . ?" She shook her head in confusion. "I . . ."

He kissed her tenderly on the lips.

"Sweetheart, I love you. I want you to be a part of my life."

Her eyes clouded and he knew she was struggling to accept his words. Of course she would struggle with this. She couldn't trust love. Not that fast. But she would with time. He'd make sure of it. But right now, he wouldn't give her time to deny his feelings. Or hers.

He captured her lips again, gently at first, stroking her lips with his own. Then he deepened the kiss. Finally, she succumbed to his tender persuasion and melted against him. Her tongue glided along his lips, then slipped inside. He groaned and gathered her closer.

Danielle knew she was losing the battle. Trey in love with her? But that's not how it was supposed to go. He was supposed to fall for Jake again. Not her!

But God, it felt so good being in his arms. It felt so warm . . . so comforting. She felt so loved. His embrace felt like a warm, safe haven. It was sweeter than anything she'd ever experienced.

He'd said he loved her. That he wanted her in his life. He would cherish her . . . and take care of her.

Thoughts of Jake and the betrayal this would mean slipped away, despite her desperate attempts to hang on to them. They simply could not survive Trey's passionate, tender kisses, which showed how clearly he loved her.

And as her heart soared, she realized how much she loved him, too.

She stroked her hands over his broad shoulders, then

down his sculpted chest, reveling in the feel of hard male muscle under her palms. He was so strong. So masculine. Solid. With him she would never be alone again. When she needed someone to lean on, he would be there.

She stroked down his taut stomach and over the denim bulging below. She unzipped and slipped her hand inside, desperate to feel his rock-solid cock. Wanting to join with him in the most basic of ways. To remind herself how well they fit together. To experience again the deep intimacy of making love with him. Of surrendering to him, knowing he would never hurt her, and she would be totally safe in his arms.

She wrapped her fingers around his cock. Hard as marble, but hot as fire. She stroked his length. He pressed her back against the bed and unfastened her blouse as he stared down at her with loving eyes.

"You are so beautiful."

She stroked him again, loving the feel of his hard shaft in her hand. She cupped the crown in her palm and stroked the ridge under the corona. He peeled back the fabric of her top and kissed the base of her neck, then nuzzled gently. He left a trail of sweet butterfly kisses as he traveled to the swell of her breasts, kissing above the lace cups of her bra. He unsnapped her bra and drew it away from her body. Then his lips found her nipple and he tasted her.

Wild sensations fluttered through her as he nudged the tight bead with his tongue, then sucked lightly. She tightened her hand around his shaft. Her insides ached with wanting him. He kissed across her chest to her other nipple and drew it into his warm mouth. She moaned at the incredible sensation. He captured her lips again, then drew away from her. He unfastened the snap on his jeans and dropped them to the floor, then relieved her of her jeans, along with the panties she wore.

He returned to the bed and kissed along her thigh while lightly stroking the other. Tingles rippled through her and she ran her hands through his sandy brown hair, the spiky strands gliding through her fingers. Then his mouth found her intimate folds and his tongue dragged along her opening. He covered her clit and his tongue dabbed lightly.

A flurry of pleasure skittered through her. When he began to suck, she grasped his head and held him to her. As he licked and sucked, he stroked her opening with a seeking finger. She arched against him, moaning her encouragement. He slipped inside and stroked her hot passage.

Pleasure swept through her as he tweaked her clit. She opened her arms. He stood, his magnificent cock standing straight up, then prowled over her. He captured her lips and she arched her chest against him. Her breasts brushed against his solid chest. Soft against hard. Her nipples drilled into him as he lowered his body onto hers. She guided his cock to her slick opening and stroked it along the wet folds. He smiled and thrust forward, driving his considerable length deep inside her. She moaned as he pivoted back, then drove deep again. She wrapped her legs around his waist, opening herself wider to him. He pivoted back, then drove deeper still.

Pleasure spiraled through her and she moaned. He thrust into her again and again and her senses rippled with acute pleasure.

His fingers stroked through her hair and he cupped her head as he murmured, "Oh, sweetheart, I love you so much."

His words blazed through her consciousness, and the swelling pleasure burst into a mind-blowing orgasm. Ecstasy encompassed her, expanding to an infinite sense of bliss.

Trey loved her!

Oh God. What the hell was I thinking?

Danielle gazed at Trey's strong classic features, illuminated by the soft moonlight shimmering in the window. His chest rose and fell in a slow rhythm. She snuggled a little closer, enjoying the feel of his heartbeat so close to hers.

He had told her he loved her. And, for a while, she had believed him. Not that she believed he had lied . . . just that he had gotten caught up in the emotions of the moment.

Worse, she had fallen under the same spell and convinced herself she loved him, too. This week with Trey and his sisters . . . feeling part of a family . . . having someone care about her and hold her in a time of emotional crisis . . . had gotten the better of her. She wanted so much to belong, to be loved. It had been natural, to believe she was actually in love.

Now she had to worry about damage control. First thing in the morning, she had to set Trey straight. Without hurting him.

That was the tricky part.

She pressed her cheek again his warm smooth chest, listening to the steady beating of his heart.

Oh, how she dreaded the arrival of morning.

Trey opened his eyes to a soft hand stroking his cheek. He smiled at Danielle as she sat beside him on the bed. But as soon as his gaze locked with hers, his heart compressed.

Something was wrong.

He took her hand and kissed her palm. "What is it?"

She pursed her lips, her emerald eyes shimmering.

Something was definitely wrong.

"I . . . have to leave," she said.

"Why?"

"Because last night was . . . a mistake."

He kissed her hand again, then held it as he sat up. "What do you mean?"

"I mean, when you said you loved me . . ." She sighed. "I should have said something then, but . . ."

He crossed his legs and turned to face her. He took both her hands in his. He could tell by her expression that she wasn't about to proclaim her love in return.

"Danielle, I love you."

She shook her head and he drew in a breath.

"I know you're not ready to accept it, and that's fine, but I do love you."

"No, you don't, Trey."

"Yes, I do. With your background, I know you'll have a hard time accepting love—"

"No, that's not it." She stared hard into his eyes. "I know I have issues, I'm not denying that, but . . . the reason I believe you can't love me is because"—she stroked his cheek and gazed at him with a tender look—"you can't love anyone else until you love yourself."

He stared at her in total incomprehension. This was about her, not him. What was she trying to say?

"Why do you think I don't love myself?"

"Trey, you don't accept who you are. In college, you and Jake were in love. No matter what your feelings are for him now, that was true then. But you don't accept that. You don't accept that you can love a man."

"I love being with women."

"But, at least once, you loved a man."

Anger shot through him, but he tamped it down. "Look, Danielle, I don't know why you're on about this, but Jake and I have moved on, that's all. We're friends now."

"I think we both know that you two are way more than friends. After all the weekends we've spent together, are you seriously going to classify him as a friend?"

"No . . . I . . . It doesn't matter. Jake is fine with our relationship as it is."

"Well, I'm not. I don't think it's fair to leave him out in the cold because you can't admit to your family what truly makes you happy."

He hesitated.

"I can't tell," she continued, "if you chose to be with me because it's what your heart wants, or it's simply what you believe your family wants. And I'm sorry, Trey, but that's not good enough for me."

"My family has nothing to do with this."

"So you're fine with telling them that you also enjoy being with men?"

"There's no reason to tell them. My sexual preference is immaterial to my relationship with my sisters."

"Unless hiding it gets in the way of being who you are."

"And who do you think I am?" he bit out.

"A man who loves a man and is afraid to admit it . . . even to himself."

"You're wrong, Danielle. It's you I love."

Danielle shook her head and drew her hands from his. He caught her wrist and drew her back.

"Look me right in the eye and tell me you don't love me," he demanded.

She gazed at him, her eyes glimmering in the morning light. She shook her head. "I can't."

He smiled triumphantly.

"I feel it—the same thing you do—but I know it's not real. The strong feelings I have for you . . . that I could so easily mistake for love . . . are just me wanting to be a part of a family. Your family. But it wouldn't be fair to pretend I love you, just to get what I want. Just because it's the easy choice."

She stood up and pulled on her robe.

"I can't stay here, Trey. You can tell your sisters I had to get home, that something came up. Probably easiest just to say I had a deadline come up with work."

"Don't go, Danielle."

She met his gaze. His chest tightened when he saw how incredibly sad she looked.

"Thank you for this time with your family, Trey. It has meant a lot to me." She stepped into the bathroom and closed the door.

Danielle showered and dressed. When she returned to the bedroom, Trey was dressed and waiting for her.

"Please don't leave, Dani."

She stepped toward him and took his hands—mostly to stop him from embracing her—and kissed him lightly on the lips.

"Good-bye, Trey." She walked from the room without looking back.

"Danielle?" Suzie said as Danielle stepped into the living room. Her gaze locked on the suitcase in her hand.

"Honey, I'm sorry." Suzie gazed at Danielle with wide eyes. "I didn't mean to upset you last night. Me and my stupid questions."

The tears now welling from Suzie's eyes touched Danielle, and, hesitantly, she opened her arms to Trey's sister. She could feel Trey's gaze from the hallway.

Suzie wrapped her arms around Danielle in a tight embrace, and Danielle accepted it. And returned it.

"It's okay. It was good for me to talk about it."

It felt warm and comforting in Suzie's arms. She would miss this taste of being part of a family. Of having a sister.

And a man who loved her.

Suzie glanced at the suitcase. "You're not leaving because of me are you?"

"No, I had something come up. There's some work I have to get done. I'm sorry I can't stay for the rest of your visit."

She hugged Suzie again, then left without another word.

Eighteen

Jake heard the doorbell ring as he stepped out of the shower. He scrubbed his hair with a towel, then tugged on his blue terry robe and tied it as he strode across the living room to the entrance.

He pulled open the door. There stood Danielle.

What a great way to start the day.

"Well, good morning." He smiled but she did not return it. He glanced behind her but couldn't see Trey or his sisters.

"Sorry to catch you in the shower. I . . . should have called first."

"Nonsense. Come in."

She nodded and stepped inside. He closed the door and followed her into the living room.

"Would you like some coffee?"

"That would be lovely. Thanks."

She sat on the couch as he headed to the kitchen. The automatic coffeemaker had brewed two cups. He filled two mugs and added cream and sugar to the glass mug Danielle liked so much and just sugar to his. He set up the coffeemaker for another few cups, then carried the steaming mugs into the living room.

He handed her the glass mug and sat down beside her on the couch. She did not smile, and he could sense the tension in her.

"So you look pretty glum this morning. Want to talk about it?"

She sipped her coffee, then set the mug down on the table.

"Last night, Trey told me he loved me."

Jake's gut clenched. Damn it. Trey loved her? And he'd told her? Where the hell did that leave Jake?

One glance at Danielle's unhappy face put things into perspective.

"I take it you don't love him?"

Her fists clenched in her lap and her face turned away from him. Her body trembled. Was she hiding tears?

"Danielle? Do you love him?"

"I . . . yes . . ." She shook her head. "I mean . . . no."

His stomach clenched. "You don't sound too sure."

She turned to face him and tears welled in her eyes. "I feel like I love him but . . ." She grabbed a tissue from the box on the side table and wiped away her tears. "I . . .

know it isn't real. These past days spending time with him and his sisters . . . feeling like I belong to a family . . . it's a very seductive feeling."

He nodded. "I can see how you might mistake those feelings for love. Did you tell Trey this?"

"Of course, but he thinks I'm just having trouble accepting love . . . because of my background. I told him . . ." She sucked in a quivering breath. "I told him that no matter what, he couldn't love me, because . . . he needs to learn to love himself."

"You told him that?"

She nodded. "If he can't face that he loves you . . . or that he did love you . . . If he can't face the possibility of loving a man . . . then how can he know if he loves me . . . or any woman?"

He slid his arms around her and drew her close to his chest. Her damp face rested against his robe and he stroked her hair.

"You've got it all figured out." He sighed. "Now what would you say if I told you"—he tucked his finger under her chin and lifted her face until their gazes caught—"that *I* love you?"

Danielle stared up at him, shock tumbling through her. She had intended to go back home to Phoenicia, but once she'd started driving, she'd felt so empty inside. So alone. She'd thought going to see Jake would help. But now . . .

"Jake, you shouldn't joke—"

He captured her lips. Fervently. The underlying passion swelled through her, blazing through her blood like wildfire.

"My God, Dani. I love you. I've wanted to tell you for so long."

Her eyes widened. "But . . . I thought you loved Trey. That's why we started this whole thing."

"No, that's why *you* started it," he reminded her. "I went along with it because . . . you seemed to want it to happen so much."

Jake didn't care about getting together with Trey? But she knew they cared about each other. She could *feel* it.

He tightened his arms around her. "Anyway, I just told you I love you. Let's not talk about Trey."

He captured her lips and she melted against his hard masculine body. His arms around her made her feel protected and . . . loved.

Jake loved her?

Overwhelming emotions welled up inside her. Warm, powerful feelings. Loving feelings.

Was she in love with Jake? Had she been falling in love with him all along? Of course she wouldn't want to admit it to herself . . . not when she wanted him and Trey to get together. . . .

Not when she never believed she'd actually find someone to love . . . someone who would love her back.

He stroked her hair behind her ears and cupped her face. "Dani. Tell me you love me, too."

She stared at him, searching her heart. Uncertainty twisted through her. Should she tell him? What if it wasn't real? What if, like with Trey, it was her need to belong to someone? To be needed?

"Don't be afraid, sweetheart. I know these emotions are confusing to you. I know you don't trust your instincts about love. Just tell me how you feel right now."

"I . . ." As she stared into his deep blue eyes, she saw love shining there. For her. She felt his heart beating against hers. She wanted to melt into him. Become one with him.

"I . . ." She raised her hand and stroked it over his raspy cheek, and tears pushed at her eyes. "I do love you."

Maybe it was a mistake to say it. Maybe she'd regret it later. But right now, with her heart thundering in her chest . . . and a yearning in her so powerful she thought she might faint from the need . . . she had to express what she felt for this wonderful man.

"I love you." She pressed her lips to his and stroked her tongue forward.

He met it, and their tongues arched together in a passionate dance. She stared into the depths of his midnight eyes. He stroked her hair back with a tender brush of his fingertips.

"Oh, Dani, I want you so much."

She sucked in a deep breath, nodding. "Me, too."

His fingers found the buttons of her blouse and he released them, quickly and clumsily. When his hands stroked over her breasts, she cried out at the exquisite arousal of her hardening nipples. She kissed beneath his chin as she opened his robe and slipped her hand inside, impatient to feel his sturdy cock in her hand. It was big and hard and hot.

He groaned and dropped his robe to the floor then kicked it away. She stroked his cock, loving the feel of the kid-leather-soft flesh stretched over an iron-hard shaft. He dragged off her blue lace panties, leaving her naked from the waist down with her blouse hanging open. She reached behind her and freed the clasp of her bra, then pulled it and the blouse off at the same time.

He grinned at her. She let her gaze wander over his tall muscular body, then drop to his impressive erection. She leaned forward and grasped his huge cock, then pressed her lips to the tip. When she licked him, he groaned again. She wrapped her lips around him and lapped at the ridge around the corona. Then she dove down on him, swallowing him as deep as she could.

His fingers glided through her hair. He stroked her head as she bobbed up and down on his shaft, eager to please him. She licked and squeezed him in her mouth. She cupped his balls and gently kneaded them as she sucked him deep.

"Oh, baby. Oh, I'm so close." His hands tightened around her head and he groaned.

Hot liquid filled her mouth. She continued to suck and squeeze while she stroked over his hard muscular butt, loving the feel of him coming under her attention.

He pushed her back on the couch and leaned to her breast. He captured her nipple and sucked it deep into his mouth. She moaned at the exquisite heat of him around her and at the deep yearning that pulsed through her at his touch. He shifted to her other breast and sucked, while continuing to caress the first.

She grabbed his cock and stroked. It was already hard again.

"Please, Jake. I want you inside me."

He captured her lips again in a passionate kiss.

"Whatever you want, I'll give you."

He climbed over her, then pressed his cockhead to her opening . . . which was wet and ready for him. He captured her lips again, kissing her passionately as he slid inside her. She felt so close to him. So loved.

When he was fully immersed in her, he released her lips and gazed into her eyes.

"I love you, sweetheart." He stroked her cheek, filling her with warmth.

Then his cock twitched inside her, sending hot rippling sensations throughout her body. She squeezed him inside her and he groaned. His long hard cock filled her so full.

She wrapped her legs around him, pulling him deeper. She almost cried out at the exquisite feeling of being filled so deeply by his hard length. His arms wrapped around her and he pulled her tight to his body.

"You are so incredibly hot around me," Jake said. His twitching cock left no doubt about what heat he was talking about.

He drew back, his cock stroking inside her, then drove forward again. She moaned at the exquisite invasion. Pleasure washed through her in waves. He drew back again, then forward.

"Oh, Jake."

He pulled back and drove forward faster this time. Her head began to spin and her body thrummed with pleasure.

"Yes."

He plunged faster . . . deeper . . . filling her thoroughly. His hard cock stroking her insides. Soon he was pumping into her like a jackhammer. Thought melted away and joy pulsed through her . . . expanding . . . enhanced by a million delightful sensations dancing through her body.

Jake kissed her. His tongue dove into her mouth and mirrored his cock's rapid thrusting. She sucked his tongue, moaning, barely able to get enough of him.

Then she felt it. That huge wave of bliss washing over her.

"Oh, Jake. Oh, I'm . . ." She moaned at the onslaught of pleasure. ". . . coming."

Ecstasy burst through her and she clung to him. He continued to thrust, riding her orgasm as she wailed her release. Jake groaned and held her tight, grinding his cock deep inside her. It pulsed and liquid heat filled her.

He continued to hold her tight against him, his hard cock still immersed in her, and she wished he'd never let her go.

Trey sat on the bench beside Suzie as they watched Tasha feed the ducklings with torn pieces of bread she'd brought from home. Tasha tossed a handful of chunks toward the babies and they dashed around, retrieving the scattered pieces. The mother duck snatched up a big fluffy white hunk Tasha tossed in her direction.

The sun shone down bright and cheerful, but Trey's heart was heavy. He still couldn't believe Danielle had left. He'd told her he loved her and . . . she'd fled. How could she believe she didn't love him back? The way she looked at him . . . the way she touched him. How could she deny her feelings?

And that excuse about him not loving himself . . .

He was sure her doubts stemmed from fear. Fear that their relationship wouldn't last. Fear of truly depending on another person. Fear of really listening to her heart. She didn't believe in happily-ever-after. At least not for herself.

He hadn't told Jake yet.

He glanced at the golden sunlight reflecting off the philosophy building across the creek. Trey and his sisters had stopped at the campus because he had to make a quick visit to his office. After that they would head to lunch together.

He stood up. "Suzie, I'll go stop by my office. How about I see you back at the campus center in about an hour and a half?"

He knew both his sisters loved shopping in the little campus shop which had apparel, glasses, mugs, and various items emblazoned with the university crest. And if they ran out of shopping to do, there was the café. It wouldn't take him that long, but he would use the extra time to stop by Jake's office.

"Okay," Suzie said as she watched the ducklings with delight.

Trey crossed the campus to the computer building and walked the two flights up to his office. He chatted with Irene, his co-worker, about a nasty bug she'd found in the new student tracking system they'd been developing together, and helped her debug it for about twenty minutes. Finally, they pinpointed the problem area—it was always easier when they put their heads together—and discussed solutions around the problem.

He glanced at his watch and realized he'd been there almost an hour. He bid Irene good-bye and headed toward the philosophy building.

"Hi. I'm ready for lunch."

Jake glanced up and smiled when he saw Danielle standing in the doorway to his office. This morning had been sensational, and he was floating on air knowing she loved him.

He gestured her into his office. "Are you sure we don't need to discuss your grades and how you can improve them?"

She closed the door behind her and locked it. As she walked toward him, he stood up. She stepped into his arms and kissed him soundly.

"Why, Professor Jamieson, you already promised me an A plus."

"Did I now?" He slid his hands around her body and cupped her deliciously firm ass, then pulled her tighter against him. His cock swelled at the feel of her pressed against him. "Is there anything else you'd like me to give you?"

She ran her hand over his growing bulge and he had to stifle a groan.

"You told me you have a meeting after lunch so we don't have much time."

She reached under her skirt and slid down her panties, then dropped them into his hand. She sat on his desk and drew him toward her as she raised her legs on either side of him and propped her feet on his chair. She unfastened his zipper and sent him a devilish smile as she drew out his rock-hard cock, then leaned forward and licked him, then swirled her tongue over and all around his cockhead.

"You're very hard, Professor Jamieson."

She pulled aside her skirt, revealing her naked pussy. His heart pounded.

"Please slide your delicious hard cock into me and fuck me."

She tugged on his cock, and as soon as his cockhead pressed against her hot slick pussy, he groaned. He thrust forward, impaling her. This time, she groaned.

She wrapped her arms around him and cupped his ass. He thrust and thrust again.

"Oh, yes. Fuck me hard, Professor. Make me come."

She gasped as he drove in deep and hard. He could feel her heart thumping against her chest, her breathing accelerating. His body tightened as he pumped into her. Faster. Harder.

She moaned, then gasped.

"Oh, yes. I'm . . . coming."

He held her tight as he thrust her over the edge, then kissed her . . . swallowing her wail of bliss as she plummeted into an intense orgasm. He thrust again and erupted inside her.

They clung to each other, his arms encircling her body, her hands cupping his ass and holding him tight in the cradle of her thighs. Reluctantly, he drew back, pulling free of the hot embrace of her body.

"I think I'd better feed you now," he said.

He grabbed the panties he'd dropped on his chair at some point and handed them to her. She slipped them on, then smoothed down her skirt.

He accompanied her to the door, then opened it. As they started out of the office, the phone rang.

"I'll just get that," he said as he headed back into the office. He picked up the phone. "Hello? Yes, okay . . . Sure. Two o'clock would be fine." He hung up the phone. "It turns out my appointment is delayed so we have some extra time."

He stepped from behind his desk and took her into his arms, wanting to taste her again. He kissed her, savoring the feel of her soft full lips.

Nineteen

Trey walked along the hall toward Jake's office and saw Suzie standing at Jake's door. Oh, damn. Was she still after Jake, even after their conversation?

"Suzie?"

She turned to face him, a stunned look on her face. Her eyes widened.

What in hell was wrong with her?

"No, Trey," she whispered. "Don't—"

But he pushed aside her feeble attempt to stop him from glancing into Jake's office . . . to see Danielle in an ardent embrace with Jake, their lips melded in a passionate kiss.

"And I thought it was awkward when you caught *me* kissing Jake," Suzie mumbled.

———

Danielle heard muffled voices and drew away from Jake. She glanced toward the door to see Trey glaring at her. And behind him stood Suzie.

Oh God, this was a disaster.

"Trey. I . . ."

But his closed angry expression stopped her.

"Danielle, I thought you went home. You said you had some work that came up," Suzie said, her voice breaking the cold silence.

Danielle glanced from Suzie to Trey and back to Suzie again. Even with evidence right in front of her that Danielle was cheating on her brother with another man, Suzie seemed to be open to an explanation. She seemed to be ready to accept that what was right in front of her eyes was not exactly what it appeared to be.

Just like a true sister would.

Unfortunately, Danielle had no explanation to offer.

She couldn't expose Trey by saying that she was the glue to reunite Trey with his ex-lover Jake. She couldn't even say that she and Trey and Jake were lovers in a sexy three-some . . . because that would mortify Trey.

And whatever they'd been in the past, the moment Trey had proclaimed his love for her, when Danielle turned to Jake, she felt as if she was cheating on Trey.

She chewed her lower lip as her heart thumped loudly in her chest.

"Suzie, why don't you go find Tasha." Trey bit the words out.

Suzie sent Danielle a quick glance, then nodded and turned around. Her footsteps echoed down the hallway. Trey stepped into the office and closed the door behind him.

"What's going on?" His gaze shot through Danielle like a spear.

She stood motionless, unable to utter a sound. Trey's jaw clenched tightly and his hawklike gaze turned to Jake.

"Damn it, Jake. Danielle must have told you what happened last night."

"You mean, when you told her you love her?" Jake glared at Trey. "And what about me?"

"What about you?" Trey shot back, sparks in his eyes.

Jake's fists clenched at his sides. "We went into this as a threesome . . . and now you want to walk away with the girl?"

As their anger flared, Danielle's heart compressed. This wasn't the way it was supposed to go.

"For heaven's sake, I started all this to bring you two together again," she said, "not to drive you apart."

"What?" Trey stared at her.

"I . . . I wanted to be with the two of you, that was always true, but I have always known that the two of you were meant to be together. I thought that maybe . . . since you both liked the arrangement with me . . . that keeping it going would keep you two seeing each other, and I hoped . . . I really believed that . . . you might get back together."

Trey turned to Jake. "Did you know about this?"

Jake just shrugged. "That doesn't matter now." He turned around and met Trey's gaze. "I've fallen in love with Danielle. And she loves me."

Trey's sharp gaze turned to her. "So you believe you love him . . . but not me?"

"I told you last night, you don't really—"

"Fuck!" He turned back to Jake, anger blazing from his eyes.

Danielle blinked back tears at the animosity flaring between these two men who she knew cared about each other. Trey clung to his concept of loving her only to hide from his fear of loving a man, and Jake . . .

"You claim to care about me, but you'll steal the one woman I love?" Trey's jaw clenched.

Danielle blanched.

This morning, she'd been thrilled to find that Jake loved her. She knew in her heart that she loved him. Deeply and truly.

But now a sickening feeling sliced through her. Rather than true love, might it be that he was deluding himself, just as Trey was? Convincing himself he loved her to hide the pain of knowing he'd finally lost Trey?

"What the hell kind of friend—?" Trey continued.

"Stop it. Both of you," she demanded. She dragged in a deep calming breath. "Please."

Jake clamped his mouth shut on whatever his response would have been. Trey grasped the back of one of the chairs by Jake's worktable, his knuckles turning white.

She stepped forward and rested her hand on Trey's arm. "Trey, you don't really—"

Trey's eyes blazed in anger. "You think I don't really love you?" Trey pulled her into his arms and practically smothered her with a fervent kiss. "Don't tell me you don't feel the passion . . . the love between us."

But she did . . . and that frightened her.

"Trey, until you admit that you can love a man, I can never accept your love . . . because I will always believe you're just fooling yourself."

She turned to Jake, unsure that choosing him over Trey was the right decision.

"Oh no, Danielle." Jake shook his head. "Don't tell me you doubt what we have."

Jake strode toward her, and she backed up a step, her hands raised.

"Please, Jake. No." She couldn't handle him taking her in his arms and kissing her. "This still doesn't feel right. If you two could just work things out . . ."

"But that's the whole point, Danielle," Trey stated firmly. "I hate to burst your bubble, but Jake and I gave it a good try and it *didn't* work out. We had a great time while we were together, but something was missing."

He stepped forward and took her hand, but she snatched it away, unable to bear his loving touch.

Trey's jaw clenched. "I'm sorry, but it's not going to work to get us back together again."

"He's right." Jake stepped toward her, his blue eyes stormy. "The time for Trey and me is past, Danielle. Now I love you."

"And so do I!" Trey interjected. "What we've had together—the three of us—has been fun, but now it's time for you to make a decision."

Emotions boiled within her. This couldn't be happening. She couldn't be responsible for breaking either man's heart. Couldn't pick one man if it meant throwing the other into the cold night, like her mother had done to her all those years ago.

They stared at her. Waiting.

Trey stepped toward her. "Danielle—"

"No!" She wheeled around and paced across the office, putting distance between her and the two men. "It doesn't matter." She turned back to face them. "*I* don't love *you*." She glanced from one man to the other, both staring at her intently. "*Either* of you."

At that, she strode out the door and hurried down the hall.

As soon as Danielle stormed from his office, Jake's anger deflated. He stared at Trey, who still stared at the empty doorway.

"Well, that didn't go very well," Jake said.

Trey glanced at Jake. The last embers of anger faded from his brown eyes and he nodded.

"Just because she says she doesn't love me . . . or you . . . doesn't mean it's true. With her background, she's afraid to love anyone."

Jake nodded and settled into one of the chairs by his round table with a sigh. "She's right, you know. You need to come to terms with who you are, and what you and I had in the past, before you can have a solid relationship with someone."

Trey gripped the back of the chair beside Jake's. "That's probably true." He paced back and forth a few times, then turned toward Jake. "About you and me . . ."

As Jake watched him, his heart clenched. Trey had come to some kind of decision. Jake could tell by the determined set of his jaw.

Was Trey going to lay it on the line once and for all . . . that he and Trey were over?

"I think we should have a little talk," Trey said.

Jake leaned forward. "That's a good idea. When?"

"Right after I have a talk with my sisters."

Danielle parked in her driveway and turned off the ignition, then headed toward the house. It had been three days since she'd stormed out of Jake's office. Since Jake had told her he loved her. Four since Trey had proclaimed his love. In all that time, neither of them had called her, or even e-mailed.

She went into the house and kicked her shoes into the closet, then headed for the kitchen to start dinner. Another meal alone.

She missed Trey and Jake terribly. She opened the freezer and pulled out a frozen dinner, then tossed it in the microwave. Over the past three nights, when she went to bed, she couldn't sleep. All she could think about in the darkness was how crappy it was to be all alone, especially when she had not one, but two gorgeous men who both claimed to love her.

What she wouldn't do to have a strong shoulder to lean on. To have a warm, tender—and sexy—man to hold her every night.

She poured herself a glass of water and grabbed the meal from the microwave. The spicy ginger noodles were tasty, but a little hot.

How could she ever choose between them? And if she did, how could she live with herself after driving a wedge between them forever?

Her doorbell rang and she headed to the door. She pulled it open and her jaw dropped when she found Trey and Jake standing there smiling at her.

Twenty

Oh God. Danielle's heart melted seeing Trey and Jake again.

"What are you doing here?"

"You didn't think we'd just leave it the way it was, did you?" Jake asked.

"Well, when you didn't call . . ." Damn, she shouldn't have said that.

Jake grinned broadly. "So, Trey, it appears the lady has missed us."

"May we come in, Dani?" Trey asked.

"Of course." She stepped back.

Trey closed the door behind them. Jake stepped toward her, and she willed herself not to step back. Because she wanted to flee. From the thundering of her heart. From the wild desire to throw herself into his arms. From the desperate need to tell him she loved him and plead with him to take her back.

But then she glanced toward Trey. Her feelings of love for him had not diminished either, despite her constant conversations with herself that he wasn't ready for love.

Jake slid his arms around her and drew her into his embrace. She stood stiff . . . until his mouth melded with hers, then she became a boneless mass of need. His tongue stroked her lips and she opened to him. His sweet invasion sent her senses into a spin.

She felt Trey's hands stroke over her back. Jake released her lips and turned her around to face Trey. He drew her into his arms and kissed her, his mouth moving on hers with a passionate arousing insistence. Her tongue glided into his mouth of its own accord. Jake stepped close and kissed her neck. She was sandwiched between the two of them. Pressed between their hard muscular bodies, the heat of them emanating through her, setting her blood to boiling. She could feel their arousal in the form of two swelling cocks. And her own as her nipples tightened to hard beads and her insides melted to liquid heat.

Grasping for some sense of sanity, she drew her lips free from Trey's and sucked in a deep breath. She summoned an inner strength and flattened her hand against his chest, and eased him away. She stepped from between the two of them.

"I still don't know why you're here. I don't intend to pick up where we left off. Nothing has changed, so—"

"But something has changed," Trey said.

Her eyebrows arched. "What?"

"Danielle, do you trust us?" Jake asked.

"Of course." Trust had never been the issue.

"Good." Jake stroked down her arms—then she realized he was pressing her arms together behind her. A clinking sound followed by cold metal pressing against her wrist startled her, then a loud click . . . click. He'd handcuffed her hands behind her back.

"What the . . . ?"

He pressed her backward until her legs connected with the couch, and she fell onto the plush fabric. Trey grasped one of her ankles while Jake caught the other. She watched Trey wind a smooth rope around her ankle in a couple of quick rotations, draw the length of rope sideways, then slide it around the leg of her end table. Jake worked similarly on her other ankle. They tugged on the ropes, pulling her ankles apart, widening her legs, then tied the ropes.

Her heart thundered in her chest as excitement skittered along her nerve endings. She didn't know why they had decided to tie her up—other than maybe to stop her from fleeing while they explained why they were here—but she couldn't help but hope that the experience would include some hot and heavy sex.

But as much as she wanted that, she couldn't just let it happen.

"Look, I already told you—"

Her words stopped suddenly as Trey popped a rubber ball attached to a strap into her mouth. A gag. Her tongue explored the ball and discovered contours and a ridge and . . . Her cheeks flushed. It wasn't a ball. It was a . . . cockhead. Her tongue roved over it; then she sucked, longing for a real live cockhead. The two men in front of her possessed exactly what she wanted.

If they had allowed her a moment, she would have protested, reminding them that she couldn't allow her relationship with either one of them to continue given the confusion of feelings between them . . . But if she couldn't protest . . . then she'd just have to enjoy it!

Trey leaned over and tucked a wisp of hair behind Danielle's ear.

"Just so you know, I had a long talk with Tasha and Suzie. I told them that I've been confused for a long time and that you insisted it would be good for me to tell them. That you made me realize I was hiding not just from them, but from myself."

Trey bent forward and planted a kiss on her forehead. "Thank you, sweetheart. Apparently, they'd always suspected Jake and I had been a couple, but it was clear I wasn't comfortable with talking about it, so they never asked. When I introduced you as my girlfriend, they said they were thrilled. They don't care if I date a woman or a man. They just want me to be with someone who makes me happy."

Jake stepped forward. "Trey and I have talked, at length, and . . ." He glanced toward Trey.

Trey stepped forward and took Jake's hand. "And we've decided that we can make it work between us." His arm went around Jake's shoulder. "I never really stopped loving Jake. I needed to explore other options, but . . . I really do love him."

Elation bubbled through her, at the same time as a dark cloud of sadness settled over her because this meant she had truly lost both of them.

Standing behind Jake, Trey slipped his arms around him and began unbuttoning his shirt, slowly revealing his solid chest.

"We don't want you to take our word for it, though," Jake said.

Once his shirt was unfastened, Jake shrugged free of it; then Trey's hands trailed over his chest, stroking the sculpted muscles, tweaking the beadlike nipples. His hand stroked downward, over the tight abdominals, then lower. He slid open the zipper of Jake's jeans. Trey reached inside and drew out Jake's fully erect cock. Trey stroked it lovingly.

"Jake is hot, hard, and sexy. Don't you agree?"

She nodded, her gaze focused on the powerful erection gliding within Trey's grasp. Trey released the hard cock and stroked up Jake's chest, then down again, pushing the denim downward. Jake pushed down his pants and briefs in one movement, then stepped out of them. He stood naked except for his socks. Trey pulled him into his arms and the two kissed. Danielle watched, mesmerized, as their mouths moved, tongues coiling together.

Jake undressed Trey, stripping off his shirt, then his jeans and boxers. They both peeled off their socks, then faced her, fully naked, their erections pointing at her.

She longed to grab each of those hard shafts and draw them into her mouth. But she couldn't. Right now, she was all tied up!

Jake wrapped his hand around Trey's cock and Trey grasped Jake's. They pumped each other, still facing her. She sucked on the rubber cockhead in her mouth, longing to suck on the real cocks in front of her.

They stepped toward her, and Jake dropped to his knees, so close that his thigh brushed her leg. He pulled Trey's cock into his mouth. He licked the end, then swirled around the ridge. He drew back, stroking the lovely cock in his slick hands. He smiled at her, then dove onto Trey's cock again. Trey's hands wrapped around Jake's head. He released the leather tie from Jake's ponytail, and his fingers tangled in Jake's shoulder-length hair.

Jake bobbed up and down, then his cheeks hollowed as he sucked. Trey groaned and stiffened. Danielle wished she could suck on that hard hot cock, but Jake's Adam's apple bobbed as he swallowed. Clearly, he'd finished the job.

Jake released Trey's spent cock, then stood up as Trey sank down. Trey grasped Jake's straining cock and he played over it with his lips, then drew the cockhead into his mouth. He stroked the shaft with his hand as he sucked on the head. Soon his mouth stroked up and down as he swallowed Jake deep, then glided away. Again and again. Jake stroked Trey's short hair as his head fell back. Trey cupped Jake's balls and sucked hard on the big cock. Jake stiffened and grunted. Trey kept on sucking, then swallowed.

Trey stood up and they faced her, arms around each other's waist. Trey's cock was semierect again, while Jake's hung limp and satisfied.

"We think our relationship might have a chance, but as I told you before," Trey said, "there was always something missing. We think we've finally figured out what that was."

Jake knelt beside the couch and slid her skirt upward. Trey knelt beside him. Each placed a hand on one of her thighs, then stroked upward. Jake drew aside the crotch of her panties.

"I still think you have a very pretty pussy," Jake said.

"Absolutely gorgeous," Trey agreed.

Jake slid two fingers along her damp slit, then slipped them inside. Trey leaned forward and licked her clit. Jake drew his fingers out, and Trey captured Jake's fingers in his mouth, then sucked. Jake leaned down and licked her clit, then turned to Trey. Their tongues glided out and connected, sharing her slick moisture with each other. They kissed, sharing tongues . . . then parted. Trey leaned down and licked her opening. Jake joined him, licking her clit. Their two mouths worked busily at her wet folds and she groaned into the cockhead in her mouth. Jake's fingers slipped into her vagina and he stroked her as Trey sucked on her clit. She tried to suck in air as pleasure rose within her. Jake reached behind her head and the gag slipped free. She gulped in a breath of air, then moaned deeply. Swells of bliss pummeled her as she shot off into a delicious orgasm.

As it waned, Jake stood in front of her and pressed his cock to her lips. She opened and swallowed him inside, then sucked deeply. He pressed in and out several times, then drew back. Trey slipped into her mouth, and she licked his cockhead thoroughly, then sucked him inside. He glided in and out, then drew free.

"Undo the handcuffs," she said.

Jake glanced at Trey and Trey nodded. A moment later, he inserted the key into the lock and freed her hands. She almost laughed when she realized they seemed worried she would call it quits now. Instead, she wrapped her hands around each of their cocks and stroked them with purpose. She drew Trey to her mouth and swallowed him deep. She pulled downward on Jake's until he lowered to his knees. He pressed his cock to her wet opening and dove inside.

She gasped in pleasure at the delightful invasion. She sucked Trey into her mouth again and squeezed him. Jake thrust into her. Slowly at first, then picking up speed. She clenched around him, her senses clamoring for more. Trey stroked her breast, and she wished her blouse and bra would disintegrate, leaving her aching nipples naked to his touch.

Jake drove deep . . . again and again. Trey fell from her mouth as she moaned. She wrapped her hand around him and stroked as pleasure swelled to incredible heights. Jake hammered into her and bliss exploded within her. She wailed as the orgasm blasted through her. Jake groaned as he climaxed, but he kept pumping into her. He pulled free and Trey knelt in front of her and drove his cock into her. He thrust deep and fast. His hard thrusts propelled her into another orgasm, with Trey right on her heels. Both of them exploded in orgasm at the same time.

When Trey pulled out, she realized Jake had untied one of her ankles and was working on the other. Trey hefted her off the couch and over his shoulder, then carried her to the bedroom. Jake stripped off her clothes and the two of them sandwiched her between them, Jake in front and Trey behind. Hot, hard, muscular bodies pressed against her.

Oh God, she'd missed them. If all they wanted from

her was to be an occasional addition to their sexual escapades, she'd take it. She wouldn't give up being with them like this for anything.

Their arms were around each other, with her in the middle. Jake kissed her. His lips slipped from hers and he kissed Trey over her shoulder. Joy rose in her, knowing she'd been able to bring them together after all. She'd been right all along that they belonged together.

Jake's hard cock pressed against her belly and Trey's against her behind. Jake slid into her, his shaft stretching her delightfully. Trey pressed his cock to her back opening and his thick cockhead slowly pressed inside. She squeezed against him, allowing him to push all the way in.

They stood still for several moments, enjoying the closeness of being so intimately joined. All three of them. She loved the fullness of being stretched front and back by these two wonderful men. Both men she loved.

Oh God, it was true. No matter how she tried to convince herself otherwise, she loved them both. She pushed away the sorrow of knowing she could never fully enjoy that love with a long-term relationship . . . home, kids, family. . . . She would not allow herself to ruin this moment. She intended to enjoy every moment with them.

She kissed Jake and smiled up at him.

"Well, don't just stand there, boys. Fuck me."

Jake chuckled and thrust forward. Trey did, too, at the same time. They drew back and thrust forward . . .

261

back . . . then forward. Their cocks stroked her internal passages. Arousing. Sensitizing. Sending pleasure thrumming through every part of her body . . . carrying her higher and higher . . .

Jake slid free; then Trey walked her to the dresser and leaned her forward to face the mirror. His cock was still inside her ass. Jake stepped beside them, pumping his cock. Trey stroked Danielle's breasts. She watched her reflection as her nipples hardened and protruded. Jake leaned down and sucked one in his mouth, then nipped. She cried out at the exquisite pleasure-pain. He licked, then sucked, and she moaned.

Jake's cock swelled and he stepped behind Trey. He pressed against Trey and pushed into him. Immediately, she felt Trey's cock expand inside her . . . almost enough to send her over the edge again.

"Wait," she said. She wiggled forward until Trey slipped from her opening. Then she turned around and faced him. She leaned against the dresser and opened her legs. Trey pressed his cock to her opening and pushed inside. She wrapped her legs around Trey and Jake, hooking her ankles over Jake's hips. He grabbed her calves and drove forward, pushing Trey deeper into her. She moaned at the same time as Trey. Jake took the lead and thrust forward again and again, his cock thrusting into Trey and, in turn, thrusting Trey's cock into her.

Trey's hands around her hips stopped her from flopping

on the floor while Jake's hands around her calves kept her steady. Trey's cock stroked her vagina again and again. The thought of Jake's cock driving into Trey's ass and, indirectly, into her sent a spiral of intense excitement through her. Two cocks were fucking her. Jake's and Trey's.

Trey began to moan. Jake groaned. The feel of Trey's hot liquid pulsing into her sent her over the edge. She wailed in mind-shattering pleasure.

As the three of them lay on the bed together, arms and legs tangled together, Danielle sighed.

"So do you finally believe that I love you?" Trey asked.

She lay still waiting for Jake to answer. Trey pushed himself onto his elbow and stared down at her.

"Dani?"

She glanced at Trey.

"Do you finally believe me? I told my sisters. I've come to terms with my love for Jake."

"You were asking me?" she asked. Confusion coursed through her.

"That's right. Why do you think we're here?"

Jake chuckled as he propped himself on his elbow, too. "Hey, man, I think she believes we're just here for the sex."

Trey laughed. "Well, that is a damn good reason but . . ." He caught her gaze. "Haven't you figured it out yet?"

"I . . . guess not."

"You were right that I was hiding from who I really am. When I took your advice and told Suzie and Tasha, they accepted what I told them without judgment. They even wondered what had taken me so long to tell them. I learned from them and decided to stop judging myself. You said that I love Jake but I had decided to take the easier path. To pursue women. But it's not quite that simple. I do love being with women, too. But I especially love being with you. Mainly because, as I've explained before, I love you."

"But . . . Jake . . ."

"I love you, too," Jake said as he stroked her shoulder.

"I don't understand. I—"

Trey swooped down and kissed her lips. As soon as he released her, Jake captured her lips. They both gazed at her.

"I told you that Jake and I had tried to make our relationship work, but something had been missing. I thought it was being with women."

"And he was right."

"But not any woman. In fact, only one woman."

She continued to stare at them in confusion, afraid to hope . . .

Jake grinned. "And that would be you."

Her heart hammered in her chest.

"So, what does this mean?"

"This means that we'd like to be a couple."

"I think that would be a triple," Jake interjected.

Trey nodded. "I guess that's true. Whatever you call it, we want a long-term relationship. The three of us."

"We want to have children with you."

"Both of us."

"If you want a wedding and marriage," Jake said, "and all of that, just pick one of us to be your official husband. But whatever public arrangement we have, the true relationship would be the three of us. Because we all love each other."

"You do love us both, don't you, Dani?" Trey asked.

She glanced from one to the other, her eyes welling with tears. "Of course I love you." She wiped away a tear. "Both of you."

It was true. And she couldn't have asked for a happier situation. She'd always known she wasn't destined to have a normal relationship like everyone else. She'd always thought that meant she'd be alone, but instead, to her total delight, it seemed she'd been blessed with twice as much love . . . and sex . . . as other people.

She didn't care about the marriage part . . . as long as she could be in the arms of these two wonderful, loving men for the rest of her life.

She reached for both their cocks and stroked, happy to find they were both hard. They tugged her from the bed and turned her around. Jake tossed some pillows in front of her and leaned her forward. A moment later, she felt Trey's cock press against her slick opening. Then she felt Jake's.

Slowly, the two cockheads pushed into her vagina, easing her open . . . stretching her . . . then slowly both hard cocks glided inside her at the same time. Both men fully immersed in her.

When they pulled back, she gasped in pleasure as the ridges on their cockheads stroked her. They surged forward again and she moaned. They stroked in and out, their hard shafts filling her. Driving her pleasure higher.

"Oh God. Yes." Bliss rocketed through her as she exploded into a shattering orgasm.

Both men groaned and erupted inside her.

She collapsed on the pillows, and Trey and Jake flopped beside her, their hard muscular bodies pressed close to hers.

She sighed happily and pushed the pillows aside, then climbed higher on the bed, tugging them with her. She lay on her back and they snuggled in beside her. She kissed Jake, then Trey, loving the warmth of them beside her.

She felt so safe and loved.

Although she knew she could face the world alone, now she didn't have to. She loved two men. And they loved her.

She had truly found her happily-ever-after.

Read on for a Preview of Opal Carew's
Upcoming Erotic Romance

Bliss

Coming in Summer 2010
from St. Martin's Griffin

J. M. smiled. So his perfect woman didn't believe in Tantra. But she had read his book, which meant she'd at least given it a chance. He was sure that with a little time and the opportunity to show her the benefits of Tantra, he could convince her of its merits.

He probably should have told her he was the author of the book before the conversation had gone too far, but he'd wanted to hear her honest opinion. He couldn't tell her now. At least, not right away. There was no point in embarrassing her.

The seat belt sign flashed on and Kara buckled her seat belt. She glanced at him nervously, then gazed out the window. He was fairly sure her jitters were less from the idea of landing than from his invitation to spend more time together.

Although she had flirted shamelessly in the airport, it had been clear, especially when she'd seen him in the seat next to hers, that she'd never intended it to lead anywhere.

Given the obvious attraction between them—and the fact that he *knew* she was the woman who he had manifested as his perfect mate—he fully intended to convince her to spend the night with him. *He* might know they were meant to be together, but he still had to convince *her* of that.

Kara's stomach clenched as the aircraft came to a stop at the gate and people rose from their seats and filled the aircraft aisle. Once off the aircraft, she knew she could just excuse herself and slip off to the ladies' room, or whatever, and give J. M. the slip. But . . . did she really want to do that?

She watched him as he stood up and opened the overhead compartment. He pulled out her carry-on and placed it on the seat.

My God, not only was he a gentleman, he was observant—remembering exactly which bag of the several up there was hers. He was a sensitive man, too. Warm and concerned for others' feelings. She could tell that by their conversation. And she liked being around him. That and he was extremely sexy. The attraction between them was blazing hot and . . . she hadn't been with a guy for a while.

As the line of people began to move, J. M. waited for her to move in front of him, then followed her toward the front of the aircraft.

Maybe she should look at this as a golden opportunity. She could have a one-night stand—something she'd never done before—with a sensational guy. And she didn't have to worry about the repercussions, like the awkwardness the following morning when they promised to call each other knowing full well they never would, or the potential embarrassment of running into each other again after breaking that promise.

Of course, he was a great guy and maybe she would want to see him again . . . but that point was moot since the likelihood they lived anywhere near each other was remote. Just because they flew out of the same airport didn't mean anything. She lived nearly fifty miles from the airport and he might live fifty miles in the opposite direction.

"Good night." The airline hostess nodded as Kara stepped past her. "I hope you enjoyed the flight," she said as J. M. passed her.

The more Kara thought about it, the more she realized she did not want to let this chance slip away.

They walked through the long tunnel leading from the plane to the gate, then stepped into the bustle of the terminal. The flow of people headed toward an airline representative who was waving them toward a counter along the side. A long line was forming.

J. M. slowed, then rested his hand on her arm and guided her out of the flow of traffic.

"Hold on a second," he said.

She nodded as she watched him pull out his cell phone, flip it open, and flick the keypad. A moment later, he turned away while he talked to someone, then he flipped the phone closed.

"I don't really want to get caught up in that," he said, nodding his head toward the horde of people heading to the airline desk to retrieve their hotel voucher, "so I just reserved a room at Angel's Inn, a small hotel just a few miles from the airport."

Kara knew that with so many people arriving all at once at the hotels where the airlines would be placing people, it would probably be hours before they got a room. There would be lines to get the vouchers, then for the shuttles to the hotels, then to register for their rooms, etc.

Oh, damn. Was this good-bye?

She remembered the warmth of J. M.'s hand on her back, and the calm that had resonated from his touch. She had no doubt the heat of his touch could elicit far more than a calming response. An electric zing spiked through her at the thought of his arms encircling her, drawing her close to his body, of those full lips capturing hers in a smoldering kiss.

She was sure he was as interested as she was, but . . . she hadn't given him any hints. With her luck, he'd walk out of her life any second, if she didn't do something. Now.

She stepped toward him and, before she could change her mind, settled her hands on his shoulders, pushed herself upon her toes, and pressed her lips to that sensuous mouth of his. An electric tingle shimmered through her and her hormones danced in delight. Their mouths parted and she stared at him, allowing the heat she felt to shine in her eyes.

At the sight of his brown eyes, dark with desire, her breath caught. Oh, God, she wanted to feel this man's arms around her. To feel his lips plundering hers. To touch that magnificent body of his.

His arms slid around her and he pulled her against him, his mouth finding hers again. His lips moved on hers and she glided her arms around his shoulders. She'd been right about the muscles under his shirt. She felt the solid contours of his arms embracing her and her breasts pressed against a hard, sculpted chest. His tongue brushed against her lips and she parted them. As he swept his tongue inside her mouth and stroked, she melted against him.

He released her lips and brushed the hair over her temple. She could feel his warm breath against her ear. "I was going to invite you to share my room. Does this mean yes?"

Butterflies danced inside her stomach. She could still back out. A kiss wasn't a commitment to all-out sex.

Ah, damn, Kara, don't second-guess everything.

Why shouldn't she allow herself to experience what could only be a magnificent adventure? Sure, she'd never had a one-night stand before, but hadn't she been the one saying that people could enjoy sex without guilt? So why couldn't she enjoy a sexual adventure with a man she'd just met? They'd talked, gotten to know one another. This mutual attraction between them was downright sizzling.

He kissed her again, his lips moving on hers in a sinfully sexy caress.

"What do you say, Kara?"

She simply nodded, unable to find her voice.

He smiled, then took her elbow and led her into the cold, snowy night. Somehow, he flagged down a cab within minutes and they were on their way to the Angel's Inn.

Kara stepped into the room as J. M. held the door for her. Her eyes widened at the large, luxurious suite.

"Pretty fancy," she said.

He followed her into the room and closed the door. She kicked off her boots, then slid her coat from her shoulders. He took it and hung it in the closet.

"I thought you might prefer to have a little space." He hung his own coat beside hers.

She stepped farther into the large room, glancing around at the soft beige couch and chair across from a cherry cabinet that probably held a TV inside. Plants and artwork gave the sitting area a homey feel. There was a doorway straight ahead that probably led to the bedroom.

She smiled. "You mean, I can sleep on the couch if I like?"

He carried their cases across the room and set them down by the bedroom door.

"If you don't want to share the bed, *I'll* sleep on the couch."

She tilted her head. "Really?"

He stepped toward her and anticipation fluttered through her. His brown eyes darkened as he stroked his hand over her cheek. Heat simmered through her and her heart thundered in her chest. He cupped her face and gazed into her eyes.

"I don't want you to feel pressured into anything just because you agreed to stay the night." He stroked her cheek. "As for protection, I've been tested recently, so there are no worries about that, but I can get some condoms, if you'd like."

She shook her head. "I've been tested, too."

Her gaze dropped to his lips . . . full and sensuous. Her whole body tingled, wanting to feel his mouth on hers. Her lips parted as she tilted her head and pressed her lips to his.

Warm. And firm.

The moment their lips met, she could sense his control . . . as if he had to stop himself from dragging her against him and ravaging her. His mouth moved on hers with a sweet tenderness. His tongue trailed along the seam of her lips, then pressed inside. She met him, gliding her tongue over his, then dove into the heat of his mouth. He tasted minty male . . . and very sexy.

Their lips parted and she wrapped her arms around his neck and stroked her cheek against his raspy one.

"I want to be here. With you," she murmured against his ear.

He captured her lips again, pulling her tight to his body, crushing her breasts against his solid muscular chest. Her nipples hardened and heat simmered through her entire body.

Oh, God, she wanted him.

A knock sounded at the door. She stiffened and took a quick step back. Who knew they were here?

"When I checked in, I asked them to have room service send up some wine," he explained. "I thought you might like that."

She smiled and nodded. He crossed the room and opened the door. The bellman entered the room and placed a tray holding a bottle of wine and two tall, stemmed glasses on the round cherry dining table, which was big enough for two, beside the sitting area.

"Open it now, sir?" he asked.

"Please."

The uniformed man pulled out a small device from his pocket and flipped up a short knife to cut away the metal foil covering the cork, then flipped up a corkscrew, which he pushed into the cork, then drew it from the tall black bottle.

"That's fine, thank you." J. M. signed the bill, adding a generous tip, then the man left the room. J. M. returned to the bottle, filled the two glasses, then handed her one.

She took a sip. She didn't drink wine a lot, but she appreciated the dry yet slightly fruity flavor.

She took another sip, wondering how these things usually went. Should she just rip off her clothes and jump into his arms? Or wait for him to make the first move?

She sipped again and glanced at him. He smiled.

"You don't have to be nervous. We'll go at whatever pace suits you."

Damn, but the man seemed to know her thoughts.

The problem was, she wanted to rip off her clothes and feel his naked flesh against hers . . . right now . . . but she didn't want him to think her too anxious. Oh, God, that had to be a holdover from her straitlaced mother. What was wrong with letting a man know she found him attractive and wanted to have sex with him?

Her gaze shifted from his eyes to his full lips, then drifted downward, over his broad, muscular chest, to his narrow waist. Lower to his fitted black jeans, her gaze gliding over his crotch, which was stretching tightly over a growing bulge. Her gaze shifted upward again until she met his silky-hot gaze. His lips turned up in a half smile.

His gaze slipped to her lips and lingered, then glided to her breasts. Her nipples swelled as he focused on one, then the other until they ached with need. His gaze shifted lower, perusing her body with intense male interest.

"You are an attractive, sexy woman." His voice, smooth as velvet, caressed her senses, sending tremors through her body.

She took another sip of wine, then placed her glass on the table. Her fingers curled around the top button of her blouse, then she undid it. She dipped her fingers under the fabric and between her breasts. His gaze was glued to her hand. She released the next button, exposing a little bit of lace on her bra. She ran her fingers along the sides of her blouse, parting the fabric a fraction more, loving the heat shimmering in his eyes as he watched. She released the next three buttons, then parted the fabric to reveal her black lace bra.

She tugged the blouse from her waistband and pushed it off her shoulders, allowing both her suit jacket and blouse to fall to the floor. As she reached behind to unfasten the button of her skirt, she was well aware of how her breasts pushed forward. She slipped the skirt from her hips and dropped it to the floor, then stepped out of it and kicked it away. Now she stood in front of him in only her black lace bra and panties, a garter belt, and stockings.

"My God, you are . . . incredible," he said.

She stepped toward him, her hips swaying, and she

wrapped her arms around him and kissed him. Her body, including her semi-naked breasts, pressed against the smooth fabric of his shirt, while the coarser wool of his casual blazer brushed her sides. The heat of his body . . . the textures of his clothing . . . the hot moistness of his mouth as her tongue swirled inside his . . . all provided a sensuous onslaught.

Anxious to feel his naked body against hers, she reached for his shirt buttons and began undoing them. She drew her mouth from his and eased back. He flicked the last few buttons loose then shrugged free of his shirt and jacket. His massive chest, contoured with muscles, took her breath away. She ran the flat of her hand across the silky steel of his tightly defined abs . . . then downward. He flung open his jeans and dropped them to the floor, then kicked them aside. She stroked over the massive bulge in his briefs and he groaned.

He grasped her wrist and drew her hand to his lips, then kissed it.

She cupped his cheek and gazed at him. "Don't you want me to touch you?" she asked, her voice sultry.

"I do, I just . . ."

"Want to keep control?"

He smiled and nodded.

"So . . . what if you don't? What if you just let yourself lose control?"

———

Opal Carew

J. M. had been finding it difficult to keep control with Kara. Seeing her sexy body . . . feeling her hands on him . . . her mouth . . . He had years of Tantra training . . . was used to keeping control of his arousal . . . controlling when he climaxed. Yet one touch of her hand and he felt ready to burst.

What would happen if he just let go of control? No matter what, he didn't want to make it obvious he used Tantric techniques. Not since he knew she'd read his book and was against the idea of Tantra. Another time, when they could discuss it. He didn't want to ruin tonight with a possible argument.

She smiled and stroked down his chest. Her delicate fingers brushed over his flesh . . . over his abs . . . toward his aching cock. He sucked in a shallow breath as she brushed over his cock again, then pushed aside the cotton of his briefs and freed his aching member.

She wrapped both hands around his erection . . . and simply gazed at it. It twitched within her grasp. She pressed one hand against his chest, keeping the other firmly wrapped around his shaft, then backed him up until he felt the couch behind him, and he sat down. She crouched in front of him and slid the briefs off, then . . . oh, her lips wrapped around him and she swallowed his cockhead into her hot, moist mouth.